SECRETS OF THE CHOSEN

The Apprentice Of Anubis

Book 4

LAURA GREENWOOD

© 2022 Laura Greenwood

All rights reserved. This book or parts thereof may not be reproduced in any form, stored in any retrieval system, or transmitted in any form by any means – electronic, mechanical, photocopy, recording or otherwise – without prior written permission of the published, except as provided by United States of America copyright law. For permission requests, write to the publisher at "Attention: Permissions Coordinator," at the email address; lauragreenwood@authorlauragreenwood.co.uk.

Visit Laura Greenwood's website at:

www.authorlauragreenwood.co.uk

Cover by Ryn Katerin

Secrets Of The Chosen is a work of fiction. Names, characters, places, and incidents are the products of the author's imagination or are used fictitiously. Any resemblance to actual persons, living or dead, businesses, companies, events, or locales is entirely coincidental.

If you find an error, you can report it via my website. Please note that my books are written in British English: https://www.authorlauragreenwood.co.uk/p/report-error.html

To keep up to date with new releases, sales, and other updates, you can join my mailing list via my website or The Paranormal Council Reader Group on Facebook.

A Brief Note

The Egyptian Empire World is set in an alternative universe where the Egyptian Empire never fell and replaced the Roman Empire. The split in the timeline happened after the Ptolemaic dynasty and the final Cleopatra's infamous reign. Instead of Egypt falling into the hands of the Romans, they fought back and gained control of the budding Roman Empire. All religions still exist in the world, but many have been absorbed into the Egyptian religion (this was common practice during their ancient history, so is something I adopted into the series).

For the purposes of this series, the Egyptian Empire spans much of Africa and Europe, as well as some of the Middle East.

I made the decision to keep a lot of the words

A Brief Note

and systems we use today (including place names like London and the River Thames) to make the reading experience as smooth as possible. If this was the real progression of events, those things would likely have been named differently.

Things I have kept are the Ancient Egyptian concept of a week (10 days, including a 2 day "weekend"), month (3 weeks), season (4 months) and year (3 seasons plus 5 feast days). The currency they're using is debens (derived from the Ancient Egyptian word for bread - something workers were often paid in). Names have also been influenced by Ancient Egyptian history.

Blurb

When Ani and Nik travel to the York Temple of Anubis to oversee the burial rites of a distant relative of Nik's, the last thing they expect is to find themselves uncovering more temple secrets.

With a new Blessed at the temple, a body to prepare, and their concerns over what might be happening in London to contend with, they already have their hands full.

Can Ani call on a favour from her mentor in order to uncover the truth behind the temple's new Blessed apprentice?

-

Secrets Of The Chosen is book four in the Apprentice Of Anubis series. It is a modern low fantasy series with a romantic (m/f) sub-plot and follows a new priestess in the Temple of Anubis, Ani, and her jackal familiar. It is set in an alternative world where the Ancient Egyptian Empire never fell, and set in alternate London.

TEMPLE OF ANUBIS
(LONDON)

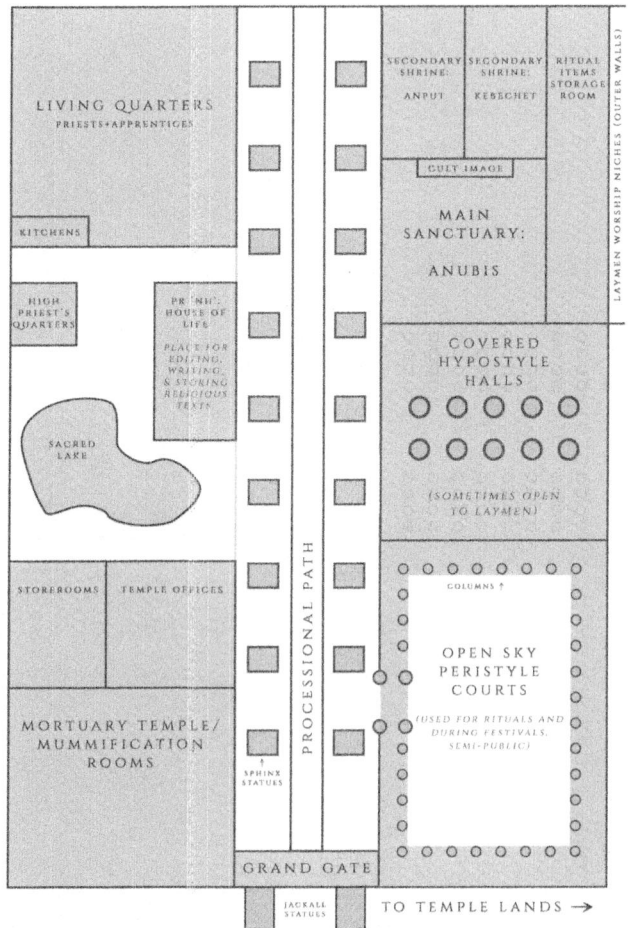

What Happened Before

Novice Of The Afterlife

With their ordination ceremony coming up, the apprentices discover that they're going to be working with traditional embalming techniques for the first time. After the initial awkwardness between Nik and Ani following their kiss to escape notice of the body snatchers, things are mostly back to normal, though they still haven't talked about it.

They also haven't found much out about the bodies that have been disappearing from the modern embalming suites, only to discover that there are more missing from the traditional body-rooms. When the bodies reappear without their amulets, they know something big is afoot and realise they have to do something.

With Ramesses spending some time in Egypt, Ani realises how incompatible they are and after a pep-talk from Neffie, she ends things with him, causing Ramesses to threaten her with career ruin.

Ani's Blessed teacher, Khafre, gives her his final lesson, with him leaving after Ani is ordained, but he promises that he'll still help her in any way that he can.

On the day of their ordination, Nik gives Ani a gift of hair beads that he'd seen her admiring at the market but hadn't bought herself. The two of them kiss, only to be interrupted by Hannu before they can talk about it properly. Once they are ordained as priests, they talk about their relationship and realise they're the last people to know they're in one.

Having realised that there's nothing Nik's father/the High Priest will do to help about the missing bodies, they turn to the only place they think has the authority to help - the temple of Ma'at.

If you want to read the What Happened Before for books 1 & 2, you can on my website: https://www.authorlauragreenwood.co.uk/p/what-happened-before-apprentice.html

Chapter 1

A parade of jackals walks neatly down the path in the centre of the temple, making me more on edge than it should considering they're the sacred animals of the god I serve.

Each of them has their head held high and the traditional golden collar and anklets that Inkaef gifted to me for Matia the first time we had a formal occasion.

I scan the line of jackals for the priest who looks after them, finding him close to the head of the parade, his pride evident even at this distance. It's an impressive display and not something I ever thought about happening before today. Sometimes, it's easy to forget that the Day of Choosing experience I had isn't the only one going on today. Up and down the country, and even all over the world, hundreds of thousands of eighteen-year-olds who hope to become priests and priestesses will be going to a temple in order to find out which god they'll serve. Or if they've been Blessed.

It's hard to believe it's been a year since my whole life changed on my own Day of Choosing. So much has happened since then.

Matia yips and pushes her head under my hand, as if able to sense the direction of my thoughts. I love every minute of having her by my side.

A familiar figure approaches from the other side of the temple. Nik notices me watching him and lifts his hand to wave.

A smile spreads over my face despite the confusing and conflicting thoughts running through my head right now. Seeing him is always a bright spot in my day, and I feel lucky to get to work alongside him.

Which is a funny thing to think considering how we first started.

"Hey," he says once he's close enough to be heard.

"Hey."

"All right, what's wrong?" Nik asks, studying my face as if he's certain the answer is *something*.

"I'm fine," I mumble, both put off and relieved that he can

He raises an eyebrow. "No, you're not. Tell me?"

I sigh and flop down onto the bench next to the sacred lake. "It's not a big deal."

"If you're refusing to tell me, then it's definitely a big deal. You tell me everything, remember?"

"Or perhaps you just *think* I tell you everything," I tease.

"You wound me, Ankhesenamun."

I wrinkle my nose. "Don't call me that, it's weird."

"It's weird to call you by your name?"

"How would you like it if I started calling you Nikare all the time?"

He shrugs. "It's my name, you can call me what you want."

"Why do you have to be so impossible?"

"Because otherwise, you wouldn't like me nearly as much."

"Or maybe it wouldn't have taken me nearly a year to agree to be your girlfriend," I retort.

Nik lets out an amused chuckle. "That's not how it happened."

An amused smile spreads over my face and I relax slightly. "All right, it's not."

"Ah, sweet victory." He stretches out, looking very much at ease despite the uncomfortable angle of the bench. "But don't think I haven't noticed that you've changed the subject. Masterfully done, by the way."

"Thank you."

"So, out with it."

I sigh. "You're going to think I'm a bad priestess."

"I would never think that."

"Nik."

"All right, but the bar is set pretty low around here with all the corruption and body parts going missing," he points out.

"Have you heard from Ma'at's temple yet?" I ask.

"No. Which is something you're well aware of. Now stop changing the subject."

"You're not going to let this go, are you?"

"No." He says it with such determination that I know it's true.

"I'm feeling a bit unsettled because of the Day of Choosing," I admit.

"Ah, you're worried you're going to have another Blessed to contend with."

"What? No. That isn't what I said."

"It's not what you didn't say either."

"Don't be pedantic. I'm not bothered about the idea of a new Blessed. I don't think."

"It's natural for you if you are," he assures me. "But it's probably unlikely. If Anubis picks a Blessed this year, it won't be in the British Isles."

"Hmm. You may have a point."

"And, even if they are in the country, that doesn't mean they're going to come to this temple. They could be sent to one of the other temples in London, or somewhere else in the country too. The Edinburgh temple has been jealous of you since you came here."

"You can't possibly know that," I counter.

"Of course I can, you think I haven't overheard Father talking to them and trying to appease them."

"It's like no one knows how the Blessed work," I mutter.

"That's because we don't really," Nik points out. "You're a mystery, Ani."

A soft snort escapes me. "One you're determined to solve, right?"

"Only because you're happy to let me." He grins widely at me. "But as for the other thing, you know you're allowed to be nervous about things like this?"

"It doesn't feel right to be. If Anubis wants to

bless someone this year, then I should support that. And it's not that I don't want to, it's just odd to think that I won't be the only Blessed one here."

"On the plus side, won't it mean that Khafre will return? That wouldn't be so bad, would it?"

"Okay, that's a convincing argument," I admit. Despite it not being long since my Blessed mentor left, I miss his presence. He's taught me so much about my powers, and that's without considering how supportive he was of me exploring my feelings for Nik.

I reach out and take Nik's hand in mine, giving it a gentle squeeze.

"You know it's going to be fine, right?"

"I do," I assure him. "So long as they keep pairing me with you."

He chuckles. "You'd think they'd learn not to do that after all the trouble we've caused."

"Hori likes us," I point out.

"Hmm. True. And maybe everyone else is just in denial because they think we're adorable."

I let out an amused snort. "I don't think that's it. I imagine most people aren't giving much thought to us."

"Even after Hannu told everyone about us kissing after our ordination ceremony?"

"Especially after that," I point out. "You're the one who said they all told you that they assumed we'd get together."

"Is it bad to be disappointed that we're not more noteworthy?" he asks.

I shake my head in bemusement. "Only you would be sad about not being the subject of gossip."

Matia approaches him and lays her head down on his leg, looking up at him with longing eyes.

Without even thinking about it, Nik reaches out and scratches behind her ears in just the way she likes, bringing a doting smile to my face. I love watching them together. There's something about it that makes me feel warm and fuzzy.

"I've never been the subject of gossip before," Nik says offhandedly.

"I imagine you've been the subject of plenty," I counter. "Just none of it very nice."

"Is any gossip nice?"

"Hmm. Maybe a rumour that you're not as stuck up as you could be considering you're the High Priest's son?" I tease.

Nik groans. "Somehow I feel like that's going to end up being more to my detriment than my benefit."

"The fact that you're nice?"

"Who my father is." He stares off into the distance.

My heart hurts for him. It can't be easy for him to know that his father isn't the man he once thought he was.

"It might not be as bad as we think," I assure him gently.

Nik lets out a hollow laugh, firmly echoing the way I really feel about the situation too. "I'm more worried that it's going to be worse," he admits. "I suppose I've always known that Father likes to look the other way, but what if he's more involved in the corruption here?"

"Anubis wouldn't be that cruel to you," I say.

Nik chuckles. "I don't think Anubis will have given much thought to my personal feelings on the matter."

He may have a point, but I'm not sure right now is the time to say as much.

"Anyway, we should get going or we'll be late," he says, already getting to his feet. "We don't get the day off just because it's the Day of Choosing."

"A real oversight if you ask me."

He lets out a small laugh. "Except that you don't believe that."

"True." I join him and take his hand in mine.

We can't, and shouldn't, act coupley in the mortuary, but we can on our way to it. "People die every day, so our work is never done."

"You've become very morbid in your old age."

"I'm nineteen," I retort, my gaze straying to Matia briefly as she trots alongside us.

"Mmhmm, practically an old crone."

I narrow my eyes at him. "You're older than me."

"By six months."

"It's enough."

"To make you an old man, yes," I tease.

"A *wise* old man."

I snort. "If you say so."

Our conversation is cut short by our arrival in the mortuary, and it's only then that I realise Nik's done exactly what he set out to and has distracted me from the complicated feelings within.

Chapter 2

"It's too early," I complain to Matia. Not that this morning is different from any other.

She cocks her head to the side as if she understands, but is disagreeing with me. Or she does until she hears a noise behind the door and bounces over to it with unbridled joy in her step.

The knock comes barely a moment later.

"Come in," I call, already knowing who is on the other side.

The door swings open and Matia gets even more excited as Nik steps inside.

"Sometimes, I think she's happier to see me than you are," he quips even as he reaches out for me.

I arch an eyebrow even as I give him a swift kiss.

It's strange to think we used to do this morning ritual without the show of affection, it feels as if it's always supposed to have been this way.

Maybe that's what everyone is talking about when they say they assumed we were going to get together.

"Did you see our assignments?" he asks.

I shake my head. "I haven't had a chance to look yet. Please tell me we haven't been assigned cleaning duty." I had quite enough of that when the two of us were being punished for leaving the vizier's funeral in order to catch an organ thief.

"Not this time. They have the new apprentices for that."

"Oh right, I forgot."

Nik chuckles. "You forgot?"

I shrug. "I suppose they don't really affect me."

We make our way out of my room, and I lock up behind us, twisting the key in the lock and slipping it into my pocket.

"And to think that just a few days ago you were worrying about whether one of them would be Blessed."

"I was," I admit. "But then you talked some sense into me."

"Ah, you mean I was right."

"Don't push it." He'll be able to tell from my smile that I'm only joking. "Anyway, I'm assuming from the fact you're not complaining that we've been assigned the same thing."

"We have."

"What is it?"

"We've been assigned to the cat mortuary."

I frown. "Seriously?"

"What's wrong with that?" he asks.

"Nothing, I'm just surprised."

Nik shrugs. "I assume they're using us to do some of the busy work while others get the new apprentices settled."

"Ah, that makes sense." And I could probably have guessed that's where we're heading based on the carvings on the walls around us. They've gone from reliefs of people to animals.

We pass the small mortuary dedicated to crocodiles. It doesn't get much use other than when one of the sacred animals of one of the crocodile gods dies, unlike the cat mortuary.

We're *always* getting cats sent over from Bastet's temple to be mummified.

"After you," Nik says, holding the door to the building open for me.

Matia takes her chance and darts through ahead of me.

I shake my head in bemusement, but really, I'm glad she gets to come with me into these places now I'm ordained and have technically finished my Blessed training.

"Thank you," I say to Nik as I pass.

He flashes me a smile that I know is just for me, making my heart skip a beat. At moments like this, I wonder how I managed to miss the fact he liked me for so long.

Or that the feelings were mutual.

"Ah good, you're here," a bumbling priest says as we step through the door. "You know what you're doing, right?"

Nik and I exchange a confused glance.

"Not really," I say. "I mean, we've mummified cats before, but we're not sure what we're supposed to be doing in the mortuary."

The priest gives an exasperated sigh, seemingly unhappy with having to take two junior priests through the job. "All right, follow me. I don't have long, I need to head to Thoth's temple, there's been a sickness with the baboons and I need to collect them for mummification."

"I thought the other temples delivered their sacred animals to us?" Nik asks.

"Normally, they do," the priest responds. "But apparently this time they can't. Something about rest days and the way things are supposed to be done. Anyway, who knows."

The way he says it leads me to believe he doesn't want more questions.

"Right. You're here for a few weeks. It's pretty standard. Mummify the cats as they come in, one of Bastet's priests or priestesses will come when they need a mummification. Then you just need to do the rights and prayers for them all. Everything's in here." He puts his hand on what I assume are instructions. "You'll also need to use the ledger to log which cat is which. But it's all self-explanatory. If you need any help, you know where Hori is."

I stare at the man, unable to work out if he's being serious or not and why he seems to think it's acceptable to just leave us without running through things properly.

Nik reaches out and places a hand on my arm. "Thank you, we've got this."

"Good luck," the priest says, already heading towards the door.

I blink a few times, hardly believing the lack of care the man seems to have for his sacred duty.

"What just happened?" I ask Nik.

"I believe we were just given our assignment."

"And no one thought we might need more instructions than *look after some dead cats for a few weeks*?"

"It is a little odd," he admits. "But we've encountered weirder."

"True." I move around and take a seat behind the desk, opening the instruction book and starting to read. "And there's nothing we can't work out, right?"

"Probably not. We're a good team."

I look up at him and smile. "We are."

"And this could be a good thing," he says as he takes a seat opposite me and grabs the ledger. "If we're more or less left to our own devices, we can spend a few weeks planning our next move."

"Which would be a lot easier if we'd heard from Ma'at's temple since making our report," I mutter. Matia grows tired of waiting for us to give her attention and wanders off to sit on a pile of linen in the corner. I probably shouldn't let her, but she seems happy there. "They said they'd be in touch when they were ready."

"It's barely been a month," Nik reminds me. "There are processes for this kind of thing."

I let out a loud sigh, trying not to let my frustration control me too much. "I suppose I'm just worried they're not going to take us seriously."

"There's no reason for them not to," he points out. "They can tell when we're lying, remember?"

"Well, the Blessed can."

"We've mostly dealt with Ma'at Blessed priests," he reminds me. "Ma'at isn't like Anubis, she blesses people every year."

"Isn't it funny how it works?" I muse. "Some gods only choose one person every now and again, while others choose hundreds a year."

"I guess it depends on what the god needs for their temple." Nik flicks through the ledger detailing which cat is which. "The ability to sense when someone is lying to them is a useful one for the Blessed serving Ma'at, but your skills aren't actually needed to serve Anubis."

"Way to make me feel useful," I mutter.

"That's not what I mean."

I let out a loud sigh and look up from the cat care instructions. I'm not paying a huge amount of attention to them anyway. "I know it isn't. And I think you're right."

"Oh, I like hearing you say that." He leans back in his chair and grins. "Say it again?"

"You're right, Nik," I repeat, feeling a little lighter than before. He definitely has the ability to make anything seem more manageable. "How is the ledger?"

"Pretty self-explanatory," he responds. "There's a coding system that seems to refer to the embalming tables and next to each of those is the name of the cat and any distinctive markings it has. What about yours?"

"The instructions are comprehensive," I admit. "Luckily."

"How long do you think it'll take us to get the hang of it?"

"A few days at most so long as nothing drastic happens."

"Like the disease from Thoth's temple spreading to Bastet's?"

"I'd like to think that most baboon diseases can't be spread to cats."

"Stranger things have happened, and we should be prepared for that," he reminds me.

"I know, you don't need to tell me." I pause, wondering what the best thing to do first is. "Should we take a tour of the mortuary? I don't think I've actually been here before."

"Me neither. You'd have thought this would be where they'd teach animal mummification."

"I guess they don't want new apprentices practising on sacred animals," I say.

"Just on people's pets."

"For some people, it's the only way they can afford to have their pets mummified," I remind him. "Don't tell me I'm going to have to have the talk about affordable embalming with you again."

Nik chuckles. "Believe it or not, I got it the first time around."

"Good. You do seem to have gotten rid of your snobbery over traditional mummification." I close the book and get to my feet.

"My snobbery?" Amusement glitters in his eyes.

"Mmhmm."

"You've never told me what kind of mummification you'd go for," Nik says as we start walking through the building, checking out each of the cupboards and rooms to make sure we know what lives there.

"I've honestly never given it much thought," I admit. "I just assumed I'd get the best that I could afford. I wonder if I even have a choice now."

"Because you're Blessed?"

I nod. "I assume everyone prefers the Blessed to have a traditional mummification."

"Huh, I actually have no idea."

"There are enough Blessed older than me that we'll know before my time comes. What about you? I assume you'll want traditional?"

"I think so. But I'm not so sure anymore."

I raise an eyebrow. "What takes your fancy instead?"

"Maybe I'll just have my heart mummified and put in your coffin with you."

I wrinkle my nose. "I think I'll pass. You can keep your organs for yourself."

"Ah, so you don't want to be united in death?"

"We'll be *reunited* in Duat," I point out. "I don't need you in my coffin when I'll be stuck with you in the afterlife already."

Nik lets out a hearty chuckle. "So long as you know you are."

"More than that, I know I want to be." I glance at him to make sure he isn't freaked out by the conversation, but he seems perfectly calm. Somehow, we've gone from barely being able to talk about our feelings, to knowing this feels like a sure thing in a very small amount of time.

I'd be scared about it, but Khafre always taught

me to trust my gut, and right now it's telling me that this is right.

And my heart agrees.

Chapter 3

The basket of amulets is surprisingly heavy, and I still have to get them to the cat mortuary. I'm not sure why there isn't a store in that part of the complex already, but it would definitely beat having to go and pick them up from the main storeroom.

At least it gave me a chance to peek in on the new apprentices and see how they were getting on. I hope we didn't look quite as clueless when we started at the temple, but I'm reasonably sure we did.

And probably still do. While the apprentices I joined the temple with are technically now priests like me, we're far from finished with our studies and have a long way to go before we're considered fully qualified. Until then, we'll be left in charge of the animal mortuaries and some of the other lesser duties.

Ibi waves at me from the entrance to the snake mortuary and I smile back at him. It's strange not to be spending as much time with the others, but it's nice to still be able to greet each other in passing. Once the current apprentices are more settled and we start having classes again, I'm sure I'll see more of them.

I lean my back against the door to the cat mortuary and push it open, trying to make up for the fact my hands are occupied with the basket of amulets.

"I'm sorry, Hannu managed to get tangled in the linen again. I don't know how he does it," I say as I enter, before stopping in my tracks as I recognise the curly-haired woman standing beside Nik. "Neffie!"

I hurry over and shove the basket at Nik so I can pull my best friend into a hug. Matia hurries over and presses herself against my leg, seeming to have missed me in the time I've been away. It's as if she's not the one who decided to stay with Nik rather than come with me.

Neffie returns my embrace. It's good to see her. Working at different temples, and on different schedules, sometimes makes it difficult for the two of us to spend a lot of time together.

"What are you doing here?" I ask as I pull away.

"I came to check the cats," she says, waving to the rows of mummified cats that dominate the room. "I thought I could accidentally run into you, I didn't expect you to be the person on duty."

"We must have the favour of the gods today," I respond brightly. "I don't think there's much change here, but if you have time, we can go to the canteen and grab a drink? Nik'll be okay here." I look at him, hoping he isn't going to argue with me.

Nik nods. "I'll be fine with Matia to keep me company."

She senses him talking about her and abandons me and Neffie in favour of him.

I shake my head in bemusement.

"Do you have time?" I ask Neffie.

"I think so. But maybe you can give me an update on the cats as we go so I can say that's what I'm doing?"

I chuckle. "All right, but there really isn't much to tell." I link my arm through hers and lead her out of the mortuary, waving to Nik as I do.

She breathes in deeply the moment we step outside, revealing a little bit of her discomfort about being here. She's never said as much to me out loud, but I know she isn't a fan of the mortuary or the way it smells.

"How are you?" I ask.

"Good. Busy. You know what it's like."

I nod, though the answer is not really. The past week hasn't been the most exciting one of my time at the temple. "I didn't realise you were going to be the one checking up on the cats," I say.

"I volunteered," she admits. "Not without motive."

"I've been hoping there was a reason to go to Bastet's temple ever since we were assigned the cats."

"Great minds think alike, right?"

"Exactly." I push open the door to the living quarters and direct her towards the canteen. She's been in the building before, but not in this part.

"Are you sure we're allowed to be here during the day?" she checks.

"Yes. It'll just count as my break." I grab a chilled water from the fridge and gesture for her to get what she wants before moving us over to one of the tables.

"I'll admit it's nice to have a moment that

doesn't revolve around duties and orders," she says as she sits down.

"Are they strict at your temple?" I haven't heard any rumours of Bastet's priests being particularly so, but that doesn't mean anything. The way a temple appears to the outside isn't always a reflection of going on within its walls.

Ours is the perfect example. Everyone thinks it's all about respecting and serving the dead, which is what it *should* be like. Instead, corruption and thefts run rampant.

"Not particularly, there's just always so much to do."

"And you have the intense desire to do it all, don't you?" I'm only half-joking, knowing exactly what Neffie is like.

She lets out a loud sigh. "I want to be a good priestess."

"You *are* a good priestess, Nef."

"I'm barely one at all."

"Then neither am I." I take a drink, enjoying how refreshing it is.

"Except..."

"Don't say that I'm Blessed. That doesn't make me any more or less a priest than any of the others."

"Not even with your pay?"

"Nope. I'm paid exactly the same as Nik."

"Huh. Somehow that surprises me."

"I'll have some pay advantages later in my career, I think," I admit. "I'll still get my salary, but I think I also get bonus payments when I do Blessed services. But it's an if-I-don't-do-them-I-don't-get-paid-extra kind of thing."

"Interesting."

"Is it not the same for Bastet's Blessed?" My curiosity piques at the idea of finding out more about how it works in another temple. I never paid much attention to the structures elsewhere. My heart was set on the Temple of Anubis even before the Day of Choosing.

"I'm not sure," she responds. "None of them really talk to me."

"Oh, I didn't realise."

She shrugs. "I think they're busy."

"Right, that makes sense." We lapse into a comfortable silence brought about by years of knowing one another.

"So, things seem to be going well with Nik." She raises an eyebrow and picks up her drink.

"Is that a statement or a question?"

"Both."

I let out a contented sigh. "Yes."

"Care to elaborate?"

"There's nothing to elaborate on. Everything is pretty much the same as it was, except now we kiss when he comes to pick me up in the morning."

She rolls her eyes. "And you tried to deny you had feelings for him."

"I didn't realise I did." The defence sounds weak even from me.

"Mmhmm. That was painfully obvious." She pauses, as if there's a question in mind that she's not sure she wants to ask.

"What is it, Nef?" I prompt.

She lets out a loud sigh. "Do you ever worry about being with someone who works at the same temple as you?"

I frown. "Not really."

"Right. Because you're a forever person," she mutters.

"I'm a what? I don't follow."

A serious expression crosses her face. "A forever person. You get the thing you're looking for, and then you're certain that it's exactly what your future is going to look like."

"I never said that."

"No? Just look around you. I remember the

first anatomy class we had at school and the look on your face when they talked about what it meant to be one of Anubis' priests. You decided you wanted to be one that day, and look where you are now."

"Well yes, I suppose. But what's that got to do with dating someone?"

"You're the same with Nik," she points out. "You realised you had feelings for him and then what? Did you hesitate when he said the same?"

"It wasn't exactly a conversation," I mutter.

"Ah, yes. The two of you were so certain it wouldn't ruin your friendship that you just kissed."

"That isn't quite how I'd describe it." A furious blush rises to my cheeks and I duck my head.

Neffie lets out an amused laugh. "That would work better if you hadn't told me *all* about it already. He brought you a present, he looked good, you kissed him."

"I didn't kiss him because of the present. Or because he looks good."

"But he does."

"You've seen him without a shirt on."

"Fair point."

"But that's still not why I kissed him," I say quickly. "It was just a culmination of things."

Including the way it felt when we kissed to avoid detection from the body thieves.

"I know, I'm only teasing," she promises. "You like him because he's smart, and good at his job, and Matia loves him."

"Accurate," I agree.

"But do you ever worry about what would happen if you broke up?"

I frown. "I guess? But not very much. We'd find a way to make it work." Though even as I say it I realise how much I hate the idea. I don't want what we have to end, even if it is still new.

"Okay, that's helpful," Neffie says, leaning back in her chair.

"Is it?" I'm not sure how any of what I've said is useful to anyone other than me.

"Yes."

"I think it's your turn to elaborate," I quip.

She lets out a loud sigh. "There's this priest at the temple that I'd like to get to know better," she says. "But I guess I'm worried that my options are going to be an awkward working environment, or forever."

"They don't have to be," I counter. "One of you can transfer to one of Bastet's other temples, and you could end up with completely different duties anyway. If you want to go for it, then you should," I say decisively.

"Look at you believing you know everything there is about love now."

My eyes widen. "What? Who said anything about love?"

"Nobody, Ani, absolutely nobody." From the expression on her face, I don't think that's quite true, but I'm not going to prod any further for fear of revealing too much. "And I'll think about what to do with the priest."

"Good. I want to know all about it."

She chuckles. "I wouldn't dream of keeping it from you."

"Excellent."

We finish our drinks and turn our conversation to catching up about old friends. Neffie is better than I am at keeping up with who has gotten married and is having children. It seems surreal to me that some of our school friends have chosen lives outside the temples and are moving into life stages I haven't even started to think of, but I'm happy for them. We each have our own paths to tread, and I couldn't be happier with mine.

Chapter 4

I pace back and forth outside the High Priest's office, trying not to let my nerves get the better of me.

"Ani, will you sit down?" Nik asks.

"Why are you so calm?" I ask as I drop down in the seat next to him. Matia cocks her head to the side and studies me as if trying to work out if I'm done being agitated.

"Because we haven't done anything wrong," Nik reminds me.

"Maybe not, but I doubt your father is pleased if he's learned about our conversations with a certain temple."

"And how is he going to find out about that?"

"People will have seen us going into Ma'at's

temple." I glance at the door and lower my voice just in case. "One of them may have told him."

"And if they did, then we'll just say that we were asked to go to help with the case against Bebi and Minnifer. Their case has only just closed," he reasons.

"And are people going to believe that? It's months since we testified about the organ stealing."

"Everyone knows that justice can take its time."

"I'd be more inclined to believe you if we didn't keep getting brought here to get told off," I mutter.

"It might just be something like talking about new room assignments," Nik tries to assure me.

"What's wrong with the room I have now?"

"Oh, you don't know?"

"Clearly not." Which he's probably able to guess from the confused expression on my face.

"We'll be moving into the priest dorms soon," he says. "They're more like small apartments with four rooms and a shared bathroom."

"Oh. I didn't realise that."

"The rooms are bigger."

"I don't think that makes up for the fact I'll have to share a bathroom with three guys."

"Even if one of them is me?"

"You think we'll be assigned to the same apartment?"

He shrugs. "It seems likely. Or maybe Father wants to check first."

I don't point out how unlikely it seems that his father would call a meeting with us for that. I doubt he gives our living situation a second thought. Come to think of it, he may not even know about me and Nik. Or if he does, he doesn't care.

"I didn't realise you were going to move out of this house," I muse.

Nik nods. "I asked to."

I raise an eyebrow.

He sighs. "We never spend any time here," he points out.

"That's because I'm kind of scared of your father."

He chuckles, but the door swings open before he can answer. We jump to our feet, spooking Matia in the process.

"Come in," High Priest Ahmose says.

I gulp down my nerves and follow Nik into the office, taking a seat on the guest side of the desk and reaching down to stroke Matia's head. She leans into my touch, giving me the reassurance I'm looking for.

"I'll get straight to it," the High Priest says. "I need you to go to York."

I glance at Nik, seeing my confusion mirrored on his face.

"York?" Nik echoes.

"Your Aunt Satiah has died."

"My who?"

I resist the urge to reach out and touch Nik.

"She's a distant relation several times removed." He waves his hand as if that part isn't important when it should be. "But the family has requested my presence in York for the end of the mummification process and the burial."

I try to contain my panic at the idea of spending time visiting another temple with Nik's father around all the time.

"And you want me to go too?" Nik asks. "What's Ani got to do with any of it?"

That's a question I want the answer to as well.

"Not too. Instead of. I can't just send you, you're barely a priest," the High Priest responds.

"I'm only as qualified as Nik is," I point out.

"Yes, but you're Blessed. They can't argue with me sending my son and a Blessed Priestess to oversee everything."

I blink a few times, trying to process the information.

"You'll be leaving in a few days," he continues. "While there, you are to do everything in the orderly fashion. You are representing me, and the London temple. I'll have no investigations into organ thefts." He looks between us as if he expects us to disagree with that.

Though I think it's worrying that he feels the need to warn us, and suggests he thinks there are underhanded things going on in York as well as London.

"Are you sure they'll be okay with you sending us?" Nik asks. "The family won't like it."

The High Priest sighs loudly. "I don't have time for the family, Nikare. What's the point of having you in the priesthood if you're not going to take my place when I have better things to do?"

Anger rises within me. I ball my hand into a fist so tightly that even my short nails bite into the skin of my palm. I want to say something about the way he's talking to Nik, but a minute shake of his head stops me.

I know things aren't great between them, but I'm in disbelief that his father would go as far as saying something like that in front of me.

"We look forward to the honour of representing the temple," Nik says through gritted teeth. "Though I believe we're due in the mortuary. Unless there's anything else?"

Pride fills me at the way he's taking control of the situation. I know leadership roles are off-limits to the Blessed, but I can see Nik excelling in a position of authority now he's shed some of the arrogance he had when we all started. It's amazing what a little bit of friendship can do for someone.

"That's all." High Priest Ahmose dismisses us with a wave of his hand. "Your itinerary will be sent to you."

"Thank you," I say tartly, getting to my feet and leaving the room before I say anything I'm going to regret.

Matia trots along beside me, her ears and tail down as she tries not to draw too much attention to herself.

I don't say anything as we leave the High Priest's residence and head in silence to the sacred lake. It's in the middle of the temple and not private in the slightest, but there's something about it that makes me think it's a special place. And I felt that way even before Nik and I confessed our feelings for one another here.

I come to a stop and turn to face him, wrapping my arms around his waist and leaning my head against his chest.

He relaxes almost immediately, the tense relief taking some of my anger with it. He holds me tightly, not needing to say a word for me to know how he feels. His anger will stem from the same place as mine does.

And then there's the fact we're being sent away from our home. I know it's only temporary, but I've barely been outside London, and I'm not sure how I feel about this being the first time.

Then again, we'll have each other, and that means we can deal with anything.

Chapter 5

Nik knocks on my open bedroom door and walks in. "The car's going to be here soon, are you done packing?"

"Almost," I respond. "Will you grab Matia's jewellery from her cupboard?"

He does so without hesitation, handing me the box that contains her golden collar and bracers. She doesn't wear them very often, but if we're going to be attending the funeral of Nik's aunt, we'll probably want them with us.

"Anything else?"

"Oh, I haven't put any of my own in yet either."

"What exactly have you been doing?" he asks with a hint of amusement in his voice.

"Stressing," I admit. "I don't like the fact we're leaving the temple."

"Are you worried about Neffie? She seemed in good spirits."

"No, not Neffie." I let out a loud sigh and sit on my bed. "Close the door?"

He makes his way over and shuts it before coming to join me. "What is it?"

"I just can't shake this feeling that leaving is the wrong thing to do."

"It might be, but there's nothing we can do about it," he points out. "Father's ordered us to go. You might be able to hold onto your position if you disobey him, but I doubt I will."

"I know. And I'm not going to do anything to jeopardise either of our places in the temple. But what if we get a message from one of Ma'at's priestesses while we're gone? If we don't answer, they'll think that we're ignoring them and have changed our minds."

"I don't think that's true," he assures me. "But just in case, we can send them a note saying that we're going to be visiting York. You can say that you're posting a letter to your parents."

"Why me?"

"My parents live in the temple complex and everyone knows I don't have any friends."

"That's not true," I counter. "You have other friends here."

"Not exactly a compelling argument, Ani," he points out.

"All right, pass me some paper and I'll write the note. This would be much easier if we had a named contact there."

"It'll all come in time," he promises, handing the paper to me.

"Just how many times have you ended up involved with Ma'at's temple?" I ask as I start to write the note.

Nik chuckles, his amusement clear on his face. "Never before I met you."

"I'm sorry for being such a bad influence on you."

"No, you're not." He leans in to kiss my cheek.

I move at the last moment and his lips meet mine instead. I set the letter down, not caring where it lands and give myself over to the way it feels to connect with him. When he kisses me like this, it's like everything slips into place inside me. I get the sense that this is where I'm supposed to be at this exact moment.

We break apart, both smiling, and I have to admit to feeling a little more settled than before.

"I wish we didn't have to go anywhere," I whisper.

He reaches out and pushes a strand of dark hair out of my face. "I know. But you need to finish packing and we need to get changed."

I groan. "Why do we have to travel in formal wear?"

"Because we need to be wearing it when we arrive."

"That seems highly unreasonable."

"I don't disagree, but as neither of us is in a position to make the rules, so we have to abide by them."

"That's never stopped us before," I mutter.

Nik chuckles. "True. But we're trying to behave until we get our orders from Ma'at, remember?"

"I know, I know." I let out a loud sigh. "I'll meet you downstairs once I'm changed."

"All right, I'll see you then." He kisses me quickly before getting up to leave, only pausing to scratch Matia's head as he passes.

I seal the letter to Ma'at's temple and place it on top of my bag, checking through everything to make sure I have it. Sadly, there's nothing else for me to do except stop putting off the inevitable and change into a formal dress.

I eye the white linen garment warily, trying not to focus too much on how impractical it is for travelling. Nik is right. We don't make the rules and we have to live by them. At least for now. And this isn't going to be the first or last time I have to wear it.

I quickly strip off my plain black work clothes and slip the dress on instead. It fits well, clinging to all the right places and giving me a flattering silhouette, but it isn't really *me*. I push the thought to the side and open the jewellery boxes Nik set on the bed for me. I quickly select a collar and bracers, noticing that he hasn't chosen anything that Ramesses gave me. I don't blame him. I don't want any reminder of the prince's threats either.

The only thing left is to put in my hair beads, but this part always leaves me smiling, especially as they're the ones Nik gave me. The ones that led to our first kiss. Well, second kiss, I suppose, but I'm not counting the first one, our motives weren't the same for that one.

I let out a wistful sigh. I'm still not thrilled about the idea of leaving the London temple behind, but I know we have to do it.

Satisfied that I have everything, I pick up my bag and put it over my shoulder, being careful not to wrinkle my dress in the process.

"Come on, Matia, let's go."

My jackal bounces to my side at the command, clearly having none of the worries or trepidation that I do. I'm glad for her. It must be so much easier to be a jackal.

Nik's already waiting for me in the entrance to the living quarters with his own bag slung over his shoulder.

"You look beautiful."

"You always say that."

"Because it's always true," he promises, pulling me close and kissing the top of my head.

"You look good too."

"I know." There's a twinkle in his eye that suggests he's teasing, but I wouldn't blame him for *knowing* he looks good. His bronze skin compliments the white linen of his kilt well, and the gold collar studded with jewels makes him look as if he's just stepped out of a wall painting.

While the lack of shirt in his outfit is fun for me to look at, it strikes me as even more impractical than my dress.

Then again, I've never travelled far by car before, so what do I know?

"Ready?" he asks.

I nod. "Let's get this over with."

Chapter 6

The countryside disappears in and out of view as we make our way down the winding roads and towards the York Temple of Anubis. I've rarely travelled this far, and when I have, it's been by boat, it's still very new to me.

Though Nik seems to be taking it all in his stride. He's probably done this countless times, though I haven't asked yet.

The realisation that it isn't just going to be the priests at the York Temple who we're meeting, but members of Nik's family too, hits me. I'm not sure when, but the prospect of it worries away within me.

The window between us and our driver rolls down. "We'll be arriving in ten minutes," he says.

"Thank you," Nik responds as Matia pokes her head up from where she's sleeping with her head on Nik's lap, having been summoned by the voices.

The driver doesn't respond and reinstates the privacy screen.

"Do I look okay?" I blurt out, touching my jewelled collar and wondering if it's too much. Or worse, too little. The politics of wearing the correct jewellery is one of the reasons I'm glad I don't have to wear it most days.

Nik barely even looks at me. "Beautiful." Which he told me before we left our temple, but suddenly it doesn't feel like enough.

"Nik," I respond sternly.

"Ani," he retorts in kind, a small smile curling at his lips.

"I'm serious."

"So am I, you look beautiful." This time, he does look at me, and I know he thinks that, but it doesn't reassure me that I look right for our imminent arrival.

"I'm asking you as my colleague, not as my boyfriend." The word still feels a bit foreign and new to me, mostly because we never really have any need to label our relationship. But I like it. It feels different from whatever complicated non-relationship I had with Ramesses.

"This feels like a trap," he mutters. "I'd like to abstain."

I narrow my eyes at him. "Don't make me set Matia on you."

He doesn't even try to contain his grin as he gives my jackal head scratches. She leans into him instantly.

The traitor. She's supposed to be my Blessed animal, not Nik's, which is something she often seems to forget.

"You look perfect," Nik says in a more serious tone. "And I mean that as a colleague."

"Thank you." I sit back in my seat and try not to focus too hard on what's to come. "Are you ready for this?"

"I'm always ready to do my duty," he responds dryly.

I raise an eyebrow. "It'd be a lot more convincing if we weren't on our way to prepare your aunt for her funeral."

He shrugs. "You heard Father, she's a distant aunt. I'm not sure how she's even related to me, but I don't know her."

"But your father must not want to insult this

part of the family, or he wouldn't have sent us," I point out.

Nik lets out a soft snort. "Father's sent us because he doesn't want to make the journey himself. The fact he can send a Blessed Priestess along with me is an extra advantage." He says it with such patience, almost as if he's not annoyed that all of this was already covered in the meeting we had with the High Priest.

"Hmm."

"What?"

"You don't think he's just trying to get rid of us, do you?"

To my surprise, Nik chuckles. "Quite possibly. Maybe he's decided we've been too quiet recently and he needs to get us out of the temple before we expose another scandal."

"Or maybe he's realised what we're really doing," I mutter, glancing in the direction of the driver. Without knowing if the divider is sound-proof, it's better to be careful about what I say.

"I don't think so," Nik assures me. "And I don't think it's really about keeping us out of trouble either. He just doesn't want to do the boring parts."

"I don't see how preparing the dead is the

boring bit." More like interesting and part of our responsibilities.

"You would say that, you're Anubis Blessed."

I shake my head in bemusement. "Aren't you forgetting that I know *exactly* how you feel about all of this? I know you, Nikare, you believe in the honour and magic of preparing the dead for their journey to Duat just as much as I do."

"Oh, I'm getting full named now am I?"

My lips quirk up into a smile. "You'd better get used to it. Everyone's going to be calling you Nikare when we get to the temple. You're the High Priest's representative."

He lets out a frustrated groan. "Don't remind me. I know why Father is sending us, but he hasn't thought it through. The High Priest at York isn't going to take me seriously. I'm barely twenty and I've only just been ordained."

I reach over and take his hand in his, giving it a reassuring squeeze. "You have me."

"I do." The smile he gives me makes my heart skip a beat. I'm the only one who gets to see him look like that.

"We'll be fine," I assure him.

"I hope so, because we're here." He nods out of the window.

Sure enough, the countryside has been replaced by the imposing stone facade of the temple, with twin statues of Anubis standing on either side of the entry.

The car rolls to a stop and the nerves spring to life inside me.

"Ready?" Nik asks.

"No. But I don't think that changes anything."

He lets out a small laugh. "You're not wrong there." He opens the car door and steps out.

"Come on, Matia," I say to my jackal. "And remember, best behaviour."

She cocks her head to the side and sticks out her tongue as if she wants to know why I'd think she'd ever misbehave.

"Nik will give you treats at dinner if you're good," I promise her.

She lets out a small yip and rises from her seat, getting out of the car as gracefully as she can possibly manage.

I follow, almost tripping on my dress as I do.

Nik reaches out and stops me from falling before I can say anything.

"Thanks. I can't wait to change into more practical clothing," I mutter.

"Same." He runs a finger under his collar as if

it's chafing. "I don't think this stuff is made for long journeys."

"Probably not," I agree.

At least it isn't raining. The classic styles that go all the way back to ancient times aren't very suited to the British weather.

Matia trots along beside me as we approach the entrance, proclaiming to everyone who sees us that I'm Blessed. Not that there'll be much confusion about that anyway considering I'm one of only a handful of women serving Anubis in the priesthood across the entire Empire.

We climb up the steps and head through the double doors. Unlike our home temple, it's all completely covered, which makes me wonder where their sacred lake is.

A middle-aged man with an air of superiority about him steps forward.

Nik dips his head, and I follow suit, trusting that he knows who the man is.

"High Priest Hunefer," he says. "Thank you for meeting us today."

Hunefer barely responds.

"I'm Priest Nikare, the representative of High Priest Ahmose, and this is Blessed Priestess Ankhesenamun." He gestures to me as he says my name.

I dip my head. Hopefully, they won't be too formal and will be comfortable with us using shortened names. Being called Ankhesenamun all the time gets old fast. I understand that it's fashionable to name children after ancient leaders of note, but it really does make for some less than straightforward naming.

"Welcome to the York Temple of Anubis," Hunefer says tartly. "This is Priest Aaru, he'll be your guide while you're here, and this is Blessed Apprentice Neheb."

I freeze in place, staring at the boy he gestures to and the jet-black jackal next to him.

Matia lets out an interested squeak, but doesn't go to investigate. Neheb's jackal isn't as well-behaved, and he has to click twice to get it to stay by his side.

I didn't think another Blessed had been chosen this year, but Neheb is standing in front of me with his jackal, so it must be true. Why haven't I heard about this already? Is that normal? I look at Nik, but I know I can't actually ask him any of this while we're in front of people.

I force a warm smile onto my face and try to ignore the feeling that I may not be as special as I think I am. It isn't as strong as it was on the Day of Choosing, but the feeling is definitely there.

"It's a pleasure to meet you Priest Aaru and Blessed Apprentice Neheb," I say.

"Hmm," Hunefer says by way of response. He doesn't seem particularly pleased about us being here.

Neheb doesn't make a sound, but that's probably because he's not had much time to get used to his new status within the temple, and I doubt he's met another Anubis Blessed before.

"If you follow me, I'll show you to the guest rooms," Aaru says. "And then I'll take you to the embalming chamber that has been set aside for your use."

We say our goodbyes and grab our bags, following the priest through the almost empty corridors.

"You'll have to forgive the High Priest," Aaru says once we're away from the others. "He's not pleased that your High Priest hasn't come himself."

"But he'd probably also hate it if Father was here," Nik mutters.

Aaru does a double-take. "You're his son?"

"I am."

"That explains it," Aaru mutters.

Nik and I exchange a glance. Presumably, it hasn't escaped any of their notices that we're not exactly qualified to be doing this. But they don't dare argue with Nik's father. Ahmose is the High Priest for the entire country, not just our temple. If he says that his twenty-year-old son and his girlfriend are the ones who need to prepare a body, then everyone has to fall into line and make sure it happens.

I just hope we don't insult Anubis in the process.

Chapter 7

"Ani, are you ready?" Nik calls from the living space of the rooms we've been allocated.

"Coming." I drape my dress over the back of a chair, not wanting to wrinkle it. Even if I prefer the simple black outfit I'm wearing now, I know I can't let my official clothing become unsightly. We still have the funeral itself to attend, and I'll need to look smart.

I head out of the bedroom with Matia trotting along beside me to find him waiting for me by the door.

"Should we be surprised we're in the same guest suite?" Nik asks.

"We have separate bedrooms," I point out. "But I guess with how few women there are in the temple, they don't have to take it into account when making their guest quarters."

"Hmm. True."

"Anyway, it doesn't matter. It reassures me that we're not separated," I admit.

"Especially with how little they seem to like our presence."

"Definitely." I sigh. "Do you think they'll let Matia come along with us? They haven't said anything about it." I lean down and scratch behind her ears. She presses her head against my leg in response.

She's only been my companion for the past year, but I can barely remember my life without her.

I glance at Nik. I can't imagine my life without him either. I certainly feel like I've known him for longer than a year.

A knock sounds on the door, pulling both of our attention to it.

"I guess it's time to go see the body. Are you going to be okay?" I ask.

He nods. "I'm more worried about the living family members than the dead one."

"That bad?"

"I guess we'll find out tomorrow." He pulls open the door to reveal Aaru standing on the other side.

"Oh, good. You're ready," he says.

"We are."

"All right, follow me." He gestures for us to head down the hall with him. "You'll find the temple is a lot smaller than the London one."

"Have you visited our temple?" I ask him.

"I trained there and transferred to York when my grandmother fell sick a few years ago," he responds cheerfully. "But I also like living somewhere smaller, London is too big for me."

He does seem to be in good spirits.

"Anyway, I'll be supervising the whole time." A hint of nervousness enters Aaru's voice as if he's worried how we're going to respond to that.

"We appreciate it," I say, offering him what I hope is a reassuring smile. At the end of the day, both Nik and I are competent, and we work well together, but we don't have a huge amount of experience.

Aaru ushers us inside the embalming room they've set aside for us, only stopping to allow us to put on our protective gear and masks.

I glance at Nik, hoping his insistence that he's going to be all right is really the case. Whether he accepts it or not, the body belongs to a family member of his. Luckily, he appears to be fine.

I take a deep breath, steadying my nerves. I don't like the idea of entering another embalmer's space.

"That thing can't be in here," a man snaps the moment Matia follows me inside.

"She's my Blessed jackal," I respond. "She can be trusted."

"She can't be in here," the man responds.

Nik puffs up his chest and stands tall. "She helps Ani perform the duties of a Blessed."

I wince. That's technically not true, but isn't fully a lie either.

"Matia will be staying by Ani's side," he continues, a firm note in his voice.

The man looks like he's going to argue, but in the end, he lifts up his hands and storms out of the room. Hopefully, he isn't about to go and complain to his superiors and get us kicked out of the temple.

Not that it's likely.

"Oh good, you scared Senbi away," Aaru says brightly. "He can be a real pain to work with."

"Good to know," Nik responds, his gaze fixed on the body lying on the platform in the middle of the room. "She's already been dried?"

Aaru nods. "We didn't want to wait and thought your job would be easier if you only had to do the wrapping. There are another couple of days to go until the last of the natron salt is removed and the insides stuffed though."

I almost sigh with relief. Mostly because it means we're definitely not going to end up stuck here for the entire seventy days it takes to properly mummify someone in the traditional way. Nik's father hinted at as much, but I never know exactly how much to trust what he says. He doesn't seem to actually know much about what's going on in his own temples half of the time.

"How long ago did she die?" I ask, looking at Nik.

"Father said six weeks. Is that correct?" he asks Aaru.

"I believe so. Let me get the clipboard." He pulls it out and hands it to me.

"Thanks." I scan down the various information included, not seeing anything unusual. Other than the fact this woman is a relative of Nik's, there's nothing remarkable about her or her mummification process.

"Have all the amulets already been delivered?" I ask, noticing the box isn't ticked.

"We're just waiting on the heart scarab. The family are insisting on importing one from Egypt. I don't understand what's wrong with a British-made heart scarab...sorry, I didn't mean any disrespect," Aaru corrects quickly.

"None taken," Nik responds. "I happen to agree with you." He shoots me a look, and I know he's trying to tell me that I'm the one who changed his mind about that sort of thing.

"I'll go check if it's arrived. I'll be right back." He disappears out of the room, leaving the two of us alone with the body.

"Things here are weird," I mutter.

Even from behind his mask, I can see Nik's smile, and I know what it looks like. "That's an understatement. I don't think they're happy about us being here."

"Because it's an insult that we are," I point out. "But they have to act like it's an honour to have both of us."

He sighs and reaches down to pat Matia. "Pretty much."

"How are we going to get through the next few weeks when it's like this?" I try not to let too much frustration into my voice.

"We'll have each other," he responds. "I brought a travel Senet set, we'll be able to play in our room. Maybe you'll finally beat me."

A soft snort escapes me. "I beat you all the time."

"And yet I'm still not sick of the gloating."

"I'm sure you are. You just want to keep me sweet."

"You're always sweet."

I wrinkle my nose.

"Too far?"

"A little. But I also kind of like it." Especially because it reminds me that I'm special. "But we should be focusing on your aunt."

"I don't think there's much that can be done for her right now. She's still got natron salts inside her and needs a few more days for them to finish up while we prepare the linen and make sure we have all the amulets we need."

"And make sure the funeral plans are right," I remind him.

"Somehow I forgot about that," he admits.

"Understandably, it's not something we've learned much about yet."

"Father is being very reckless with the reputation of the temple." Discomfort flits across Nik's face.

I glance at the door to make sure no one is coming through and interrupting our moment. Sure that we're alone, I reach out and rub his back to try and comfort him.

"We'll manage," I promise. "I don't know how, but we will."

"I know. We're capable of anything we set our minds to."

"Exactly. And it'll be a useful experience to take back to London with us. Your father is probably either expecting us to do a good job, or he's hoping that because it's for family, no one will complain too much if it goes wrong."

"You're probably right. But let's try not to test that last theory. Let's just focus on doing the best job we can."

"Always," I promise him, and I have no intention of letting him down.

Chapter 8

Nik takes my hand in his and gives it a reassuring squeeze. No doubt he can sense how nervous I am about the prospect of meeting his family. Matia trots along beside us, holding her head up high and looking every part the Blessed jackal that she is.

"It'll be okay," he assures me.

I let out a small laugh. "I don't even know why I'm nervous when I've already met your parents."

"Because you always want to make a good impression, and you're worried that people will expect too much of you just because you're Blessed."

"I hate it when you're right," I murmur.

"Would it help if I reminded you that you're

meeting my family as my girlfriend, not as a Blessed Priestess?"

"Eurgh, no, that's worse. I've only met a boyfriend's extended family once, and it was a bit different."

"Why?"

"Because I already knew them. They lived down the street from us when we were growing up and everyone expected Ali and me to end up together."

Nik lets out a snort, then covers his face with his hand.

"What's funny?"

"Ani and Ali? Really?"

I roll my eyes. "I think that's one of the reasons everyone expected us to get together. They thought it was cute."

"You don't sound too sure."

I shrug. "How can you be sure about someone who told you they preferred someone else while they were breaking up with you."

He winces. "Ouch."

"It almost makes me feel sorry for Ramesses."

"You didn't tell him you had feelings for me, did you?"

"Absolutely not. I said I had to focus on my career."

"Ooof, that's harsh."

"Well it didn't seem like a good idea to tell him that I didn't miss him while he was in Egypt."

"Maybe you wouldn't miss me if I was somewhere else," Nik responds.

"I missed you when we were avoiding each other and I still saw you every day."

"That's almost sweet," he responds.

I shrug. "It's true. I hated it."

"Me too."

"We're here," he says, gesturing to a small house on the side of a cobbled street. "You ready?"

"I'd rather face an entire temple full of corrupt priests harvesting organs," I murmur.

"You'll be fine," he assures me. "You're not alone. And you have Matia."

"Have I ever mentioned how nice it is to be able to bring her with me most of the time?"

"Only on a dozen different occasions," he quips. "Luckily for you, I agree." He pulls a treat out of his pocket and holds it out to the jackal. She takes it from him and chomps happily.

"You spoil her."

"And she loves it."

"You're lucky she behaves." I can't say it with a straight face, especially as he's well aware of how much I like the bond the two of them share. "But we're stalling."

Nik takes a deep breath. "I know." He knocks on the door, holding onto my hand more tightly than ever.

It seems he's the one that needs reassuring now. It's nice to know that I can offer him some of the same support he offers me. At times like this, it feels as if we're truly a team.

The door swings open and a portly woman in her fifties answers. "Nikare, we thought you'd gotten lost, come in, come in." She waves us through the front door. "And who is this?" she asks him.

"This is my girlfriend, Ani," he says. "And this is Inenek, she's Mother's sister."

"It's a pleasure to meet you," I say.

"Likewise. Your mother mentioned you had a friend, but I didn't realise she was a girlfriend," Inenek says to Nik.

"It's a reasonably new development," he responds.

Matia pushes through the two of us and happily looks up at the woman, seeming to enjoy the idea of new people to fuss her.

"A jackal?" Understanding dawns on her face.

"Ani is a Blessed Priestess," Nik supplies just in case.

"Good, good. I'm glad your father sent you even if it would have been better for him to come himself," Inenek says.

An uncomfortable expression crosses Nik's face.

"I believe High Priest Ahmose had some important duties he wasn't able to get out of," I say in an attempt to smooth things over.

"Hmm, well a Blessed isn't a bad thing for dead Satiah," she muses.

"We're giving her the best care possible," I promise.

"I have no doubt of that, I know how hard Nikare here works. He pretends he doesn't, but he's always tried hard at everything he attempts."

"I know," I assure her. "I was lucky enough to get partnered with him when we were starting to learn about mummification."

Nik chuckles. "Or unlucky."

"I think it turned out nicely," I admit.

Inenek smiles broadly. "I can see why you like her, Nikare. Now come, you should meet everyone else. They're sure to have lots of questions for you. Nikare, make sure you do the rounds." She puts a hand on my back and draws me into a room bursting with people.

I get lost in a barrage of names and questions, while Matia sticks to my side as if held there by embalming resin. I'm surprised. She's normally the kind of jackal who loves being around people as much as she can. Maybe it's because there are so many strangers around.

I see my chance to escape when Inenek gets distracted by an older man whose name I've forgotten.

"Come on, Matia," I whisper, hurrying away to where Nik is chatting to an elderly lady.

"Ah, you've escaped," he says when he sees me.

I offer him a small smile. "It's a big family."

The old lady chuckles. "A big family is the best kind. You must be Ankhesenamun."

"I am, but I normally go by Ani," I respond.

"Ah, Nikare's girl. He's been telling me all about you," she responds.

"All good things, I hope."

She taps the side of her nose knowingly and I let out a small nervous laugh.

"Are you going to introduce me, Nikare?" she asks, fixing him with a disapproving expression.

"Ani, this is Henutsen, my mother's mother," he says.

"It's an honour to meet you." I dip my head, not really knowing what else to do.

"You're a priestess with our Nik," she says.

"I am. This is my jackal, Matia."

"Hmm, a Blessed. You did well for yourself, Nikare. You should make sure you treat her well so she doesn't run away from you."

My eyes widen.

"I have every intention to," he promises, giving me a sweet smile.

"And I hope you're looking after Satiah well. She's passed to Duat earlier than any of us intended her to," Henutsen says.

"We're doing our best," Nik assures her.

"Hmm. But your father didn't deem this important enough to come for."

I'm starting to spot a theme in the conversations we've been having over and over this evening.

Nik's uncomfortable expression says he's noticed too, and he hates it. I wish I could do something to take the tension away.

"Ah, well. We knew this about him when your mother married him," Henutsen says offhandedly.

"Knew what?" Nik asks, his voice somewhere between intrigue and horror.

"That he would do everything he could to get out of doing his duty," she responds. "I was surprised when he became High Priest, it seems like a lot of work for him."

"Do you think he cut corners to do it?" Nik asks.

"How should I know? I don't understand anything about your temple politics. I've been a housewife my entire life," she responds, changing the subject to the food on display.

I nod in the right places, and keep an eye on Nik to make sure he's dealing with all of this okay. He seems fine, but I can tell he's exhausted from having to keep a smile on his face. While I know he agrees with some of what his family are saying about his father, it can't be nice to hear it so many times.

It isn't until the front door shuts behind us on the way out that I finally let out a long relieved breath.

"That bad?" Nik asks.

"You tell me. They do *not* like your father."

"Not particularly, no. I've always had the impression that they didn't, but this is the first time they've actually said anything to me."

"Are you going to tell your father?"

"What's the point? He doesn't care anyway."

The sadness in his voice breaks my heart. I reach out and place a hand on his arm, pulling us to a stop.

"I'm sorry," I whisper.

"Don't be. It isn't your fault I'm having to face something I think I've always known. My father isn't a good leader, nor is he a particularly good man."

"He's not a bad one either," I point out. "Just ineffective."

He grimaces. "Somehow, that's worse. If he was bad, I'd feel justified being angry at him for all of this. But his indifference makes it hard. He doesn't even care how I feel."

"Oh, Nik." I step close to him and wrap him up in my arms while Matia leans against the back of his legs. It's enough to make me a little teary, but I blink them away, knowing that I need to be strong for him right now.

Sometimes it's easy to forget how personal the investigation into the temple is for Nik, but moments like this really drive it home.

I'm going to do better at helping him through it, even if I'm not exactly sure how.

Chapter 9

"Will you hand me a new piece of linen?" Nik asks.

I pick up one of the long strips and hand it to him. He takes it from me and drapes it across the table in front of him.

He hands out a paintbrush to me. "Want to do the honours?"

I nod and take it from him. "But only if you have a copy of the passage we're supposed to be transcribing. You know I don't have the Book of the Dead memorised."

He chuckles. "I don't think you're supposed to. There are priests especially for that."

"And don't they normally do this?" I ask, gesturing to the linen we're supposed to be decorating with words from the Book of the Dead.

"Yes. I think it's the way High Priest Hunefer is punishing us for being here."

"I'm really fed up of politics," I mutter. "Everything seems to be about it."

He looks at me with disbelief clear on his face. "Did you not know that before you entered the temple?"

"I could say something about the fact I didn't know I was going to serve Anubis before the Day of Choosing?"

"Pfft. That isn't going to work on me. I know you wanted to serve Anubis even before he chose you."

"Why do you have to be a good listener?"

"You realise most people would be glad that their partner listened to them, right?"

I flash him a bemused smile. "You know I'm grateful for it really." I check the page from the Book of the Dead and dip my brush into the specially prepared ink. "Do you think I'm doing a bad job as a Blessed?" I ask.

He freezes. "Whatever makes you think that?"

I chew on my bottom lip while I trace the outline of the *ka* onto the linen, starting with the bird-like body and moving onto the human head while I think about the best way to voice what I'm thinking.

"Ani?" The worry in his voice is touching.

I take a deep breath. I know he isn't going to judge me for how I feel, but it's still difficult to admit out loud.

I check over my shoulder to make sure we're still alone in the room. The last thing I want is for someone to overhear us and think that I'm not to be trusted with my job.

"Anubis is one of the gods who only rarely picks a Blessed, right?" I already know the answer, just like he does, but sometimes it helps to say things out loud so he understands what my thought process is.

"Mmhmm."

"And he picked me at last year's Day of Choosing."

"He did," Nik responds slowly. "Much to the dismay of my father. I think he planned on me being the Blessed one."

"Anubis probably realised you wouldn't need any help getting into the temple," I point out.

"Oh, I know. I already came to that conclusion," he says.

"Whereas your father would never have offered me a place if I hadn't been Blessed." A hint of sadness enters my voice. I worked really hard to get good grades at school so I could still be considered for Anubis' temple, but it would have all been for nothing if I hadn't gotten lucky.

No. Not lucky. Blessed. There's a difference, and I need to remember that.

"True. But hopefully, he'll reconsider his stance of priestesses now you're proving yourself," Nik says hopefully. "He mentioned something to that effect the day we started as apprentices, but I've never heard him talk about it since."

A soft snort escapes me. I believe that Nik wants that, but he's in the minority. "He probably assumes anything good I do is just because I'm Blessed and not because I work hard. But that's beside the point."

"Right, sorry. I got sidetracked."

I set down my brush and turn to face him, knowing that this is a safe place. When I'm with him, I'm with my best friend. I'm not sure exactly when it happened, probably at some point between us uncovering the organ trafficking, and us discovering there were bodies going missing in the temple, but that's what he is to me, just in a different way than Neffie is.

"What if Anubis has chosen another Blessed in

the British Isles because he doesn't think I'm doing a good job," I blurt. "That can be the only reason."

"That's not true." Nik setting down his own brush and looking at me with intense scrutiny on his face. "Maybe Anubis realises how much you're having to deal with at our temple and knew he needed someone else for something here."

"Maybe," I murmur, but somehow that doesn't feel quite right.

"But?" he prompts.

"I don't know," I admit. "Something feels off about the situation. I have to assume it's because Anubis is displeased with me."

He raises a disbelieving eyebrow. "You think Anubis is displeased with you?"

"There's no other explanation, Nik."

"That's hardly true. I know you're Blessed, but even you can't pretend to know the will of the gods. For whatever reason, Anubis has seen fit to send a Blessed to this temple as well as ours. He will know the reason for that and we can't pretend that we will ever understand why."

"You make a lot of sense when you talk like that."

"Of course I do," he says. "I've had a year of thinking about all of this."

Matia pushes her head against my hand and makes a small whimper, almost breaking my heart in the process. I'm not sure how much she understands, but it feels like she knows exactly what I'm feeling and wants to reassure me that she doesn't think I'm failing as a Blessed.

"But I do understand why you're feeling that way," Nik admits softly. "I felt that way when you were Blessed."

"You did?" Surprise floods through me. I know he probably expected to be Blessed, and was no doubt disappointed when I was and he wasn't, but he's never said anything about it before.

"Well, not the exact same way because I wasn't Blessed beforehand. But Father was so convinced that I was going to be Blessed that I started to hope for it myself. And then you came along. It made me feel as if I'd done something to displease Anubis."

"You haven't," I assure him quickly, certain it's true, but not knowing *how* I know it. I suppose Khafre did say that my Blessed Sense would get stronger as I learn more about it. Maybe it's just that.

"I know that now. He sent me you," Nik says.

I let out a small laugh, feeling some of the

tension leave me. "I thought you just said you were annoyed that I came along."

"I was. And I was determined to hate you."

"What changed your mind?" I cock my head to the side, curious to hear his answer.

"Remember the first time we got paired up to work on a body?" he asks.

"How could I forget?"

A small smile spreads over his face. "You told me that I had to shut up and accept that you were either as good as I was, or we were both equally bad."

"That's when you started liking me?" I'm surprised, I didn't realise it was that early.

"It was when I started respecting you as a priestess. I'm not sure exactly when I started liking you as a friend."

"And as more than a friend?" I'm not sure I really want to know the answer to that one. It feels like it might have the ability to make me feel guilty for not realising how I felt sooner.

"I think that just came gradually, there wasn't a specific point."

"Huh."

"You seem surprised?"

"We've just never talked about it before," I respond.

"No, but you seemed like you needed to hear it today."

I reach out and touch his arm gently. "Thank you."

The door creaks open and I pull my hand back. I'm not sure how much the priests here know about the two of us, but I don't want them to think we're not taking our jobs seriously.

I glance down at the almost blank linen in front of us. They might not be wrong.

Nik picks up his brush and starts painting again as a couple of them enter and start preparing their own burial shrouds. I join him, neither of us saying a word as we focus on the job at hand. While we have a private room for embalming, we have to use the general preparation rooms that don't have anything to do with the bodies themselves.

Several people come and go, not paying us much attention. I mostly ignore them, not seeing any point in engaging when they don't want us here.

Matia makes a funny noise and I look up to find Neheb and his jackal entering the room, followed by one of the older priests who I assume is acting as his temporary mentor until his proper Blessed tutor gets here.

Then again, Khafre said he was ending my lessons so he was ready to teach a new Blessed.

My eyes widen. Khafre is going to be coming here. If I'm lucky, it'll be before I leave and I'll get to see my mentor again. Even though it hasn't been long since I last saw him, I've missed his steady presence around me.

Neheb's jackal spies Matia and comes rushing over.

"Pakham, no," Neheb responds sharply.

"He's okay," I assure him. "Matia's well-behaved."

My jackal holds up her head, as if proud of what I'm saying.

"He should know better," the older priest says. "Control him."

Neheb almost looks scared as he leans forward and grabs his jackal's collar.

Pakham lets out a low growl, as if he's unhappy about being manhandled that way. I don't blame him, and I don't think Matia would like it either.

I watch in horror as he drags the jackal backwards, wanting to step in, but knowing that I need to hold my tongue while the angry older priest is around.

But once our work for the day is done, I'm going to find Neheb and offer to teach him some things that might help him bond with his jackal and better control for both of them. I know it isn't my place, and Khafre will do a much better job, but considering my mentor took so long to arrive at the London Temple after my Day of Choosing, it might still be a while until that happens.

And it'll be good to form a better connection with Neheb. We'll cross paths in the future whenever there's something that requires all the Blessed to convene.

Working as a priest in Anubis' temple requires teamwork, and I'm going to prove myself worthy of the title of priestess, even if I'm worried about what my god might feel about me.

Chapter 10

I stare at the body of Nik's distant Aunt Satiah, trying to work out the best way to wrap her. I only have a limited experience when it comes to actually performing it, and most of it is in an assistance capacity. Which doesn't help us now.

"We have to do it," I say quietly. "Do we know what she wanted?"

Nik nods and holds out the clipboard for me.

I lift up the top sheet of notes and study the diagram on the second, letting out a small groan. "One of the most complicated styles."

"Mmhmm. She probably thought Father was the one who was going to do this and planned with that in mind."

"Or it's nothing to do with her and this is what

your family themselves want," I point out. I've seen it multiple times. People disregard the wishes of their relatives because they think they know better all the time. Normally, they don't. And I don't think Anubis minds which style of wrapping a person has when they arrive in the afterlife, all that matters is that they've been treated with respect and dignity.

Then again, the quality of amulets matters, so maybe I'm wrong.

"Maybe it's their way of testing Father," Nik mutters.

"I doubt it, if that was the case then surely they'd have contacted the temple and told them there was a mistake when they realised it was going to be you doing the wrapping." From what I saw from his family the other evening, I'd say that they hold a lot of affection for Nik.

"Hmm."

"Where do we even begin?" I ask Nik. "Have you ever helped someone with this?"

He shakes his head.

"Right." I stare at the body. "Well we know we need to wrap each of her fingers and toes separately, so let's start with that. It looks like they've already applied the first layer of resin for us too." I wish the priests who were doing this kind of thing actually told us what they did so we could act accordingly, but it seems as if we're being tested by them leaving the body in various states and we have to guess what happens next.

We're lucky we're observant and have paid enough attention in our lessons to be able to make sense of it all. Though we've never done this level of mummification before, not even as assistants. They mostly let us help with the lowest tier of traditional mummification and for good reason considering our lack of experience.

I don't wait for Nik to respond and pick up one of the long linen strips that we prepared for ourselves over the past few days.

Carefully, I start winding it around the woman's thumb, making sure it's tight enough that it maintains the shape, but not too tight that it'll cause damage to the bones beneath. I've heard horror stories of that happening and don't want to be the reason Satiah arrives in the afterlife unable to use her thumb.

Nik watches me for a moment, but ultimately decides what I'm doing must be right as he starts the same process on the opposite side of the body. We work in silence, both of us focused on the important task at hand. While technically there's nothing wrong with talking while we work, some parts of the process feel like they should be observed in respectful silence.

We really shouldn't be doing this for the first time on a body this important. This is why we normally practise on people who have signed up for the teaching program in order to get money off their mummification. It's a popular option, and I'm not surprised given the costs of some of the services we provide.

Sweet perfumes rise into the air as we disturb different parts of the bodies, coming from the wads of linen inside her. It's such a different scent than the chemical one that occurs when we use modern embalming techniques, and I have to say I prefer it, even if the woman looks less like she did in life. The priests responsible for shaping and sculpting the body have done a decent job of making her look like she had, but their talents are limited by the effects of the natron salt and the thin layer of resin.

It takes us longer than I would expect, but eventually, we come to the point where each of the woman's limbs is individually bound.

We step back and examine our handiwork. Even I can barely tell which parts I did and which

Nik did. We've worked well together since the very first time we were paired, and it shows.

The door opens and Aaru steps inside, greeting us both with a slight incline of his head.

Matia lazily opens an eye from where she's sitting at the other end of the room but ends up closing it almost straight away. I think she's bored. At home, she normally has more of a free reign, and a toy or two to play with.

And, of course, treats coming out of Nik's pockets at regular intervals. But I've noticed he's being more careful when we're in the work areas here.

"This is good work," Aaru says as he inspects the body and the wrappings. "But it isn't quite the way I'd have done it, I wonder if you're taught differently in London now."

Nik and I exchange a worried glance. It's not going to take him long to realise that we're just not experienced enough and are only guessing at how this should be done.

"How long have the two of you been priests?" he asks.

"About two months," I admit.

His eyebrows shoot up. "Two months," he

repeats. "I have to admit I'm impressed. I would have said you'd been doing this for a lot longer."

"But you said that you wouldn't have done it this way," I counter.

"I wouldn't have, but to say you only have a year's worth of apprentice experience, and two months as priests, I think it's a good start. Would you mind if I showed you the next stages?"

"I'd like that," I say quickly. Aaru may prefer a small city to live in, but he has a lot more experience than the two of us put together, and I'm keen to learn from him.

Nik nods along. I'm not surprised. Like me, he's probably realised that it's an advantage for the two of us to get some dedicated time with a priest on this.

"You've started this well," he says, gesturing to the hands. "You're fine through the elbows too, but only because she's a woman."

"Because of the arm positions," I say, realising what he's talking about.

Aaru smiles, seeming to appreciate that I'm already working out what he's saying. "Exactly. If this was the body of a man who needed his arms crossing over his body, you wouldn't be able to do it without causing some damage. Which is something we definitely want to avoid. Now, we need to use the table to lift the body so we can slide the linen sheet underneath," he says.

My eyes widen. "The table?"

"Has no one shown you this?" Aaru's surprise comes through his voice. "One of the London temples was one of the first to install them, I'm surprised you haven't seen it. Though maybe they haven't gotten around to doing them in the main temple yet." He flicks a button on the side of the table and a small whirring sound fills the air.

Slowly, the body rises into the air.

"All right, spread the linen out," Aaru says. "Make sure that you have an even amount on both sides."

Nik moves first, unfolding it and passing it under the body towards me, though I'm still a little distracted by the way the body is being lifted without any input from other priests. It makes sense that someone has come up with a way to do it, otherwise you need a lot more people per body, but for the most part, we just all help each other when it's time to pass the linen under the body.

Then again, our temple is a lot bigger than the one here, we probably have the manpower to actually achieve that.

"Step back," Aaru instructs, then presses the button again. The body lowers just as slowly until it's flush with the table again.

"But won't the straps holding the body up get in the way now?" I ask.

Aaru nods. "But we can remove them here." He flicks another switch and there's a snapping sound. "Now we need to cut the linen."

He grabs a pair of scissors from the appliance table. I watch intently as he cuts down the linen creating strips that are still attached under the back of the body. It's an interesting technique, but I'm not sure how I feel about it. Sometimes, shortcuts are necessary to make things work better, but this is one I'm not as keen on, and I can't explain why, even to myself.

Not that I'm going to say anything about it. This is clearly the way they do things in York, and while I don't think I'll be taking this technique back to London with me, it's still useful to know. Especially if I do end up needing to do a traditional mummification on my own. I hope I never do, but stranger things have happened in my short time working at the temple.

Aaru works quickly, but always makes sure to show us what we're supposed to be doing. He's a good teacher, and someone I wouldn't mind talking to more to see if there are other things I can learn from him.

"Is Hori still at your temple?" he asks as he slips one of the amulets into place amongst the wrappings.

"He is," Nik responds.

"Did he teach you too?"

A smile stretches across Aaru's face. "Oh no, we were apprentices at the same time. It must have been nearly fifteen years ago. Everyone used to say he was the one who would do well in the temple hierarchy as he was top of the class. Did you say he was training you?"

"Yes, he's in charge of training now."

"That's a good stepping stone. A lot of the High Priests have held that position."

Nik freezes. "Father never said."

"Oh, High Priest Ahmose never went into a training career. I don't think he had the patience to deal with people," Aaru says, then seems to realise who he's talking to. "I don't mean to say..."

"It's fine," Nik assures him quickly. "I won't repeat it outside this room."

Aaru sighs with relief. "Thanks. You're not what I expected from High Priest Ahmose's son."

"I'll take that as a compliment," Nik responds, and I know he's telling the truth.

I flash him a reassuring smile, wishing I was closer so I could touch him, but being glad that we don't need to wear masks now we've finished with the natron salt part of the mummification.

"I think we're ready for the resin now," Aaru says. "Have you done this bit before?"

I shake my head. "We've prepared it, but never applied it. They'd already put it on the body earlier too."

"Hmm." Aaru doesn't seem impressed, though I can't tell whether it's because other priests are overstepping, or because we've been sent to do something that we can't actually do yet. "We can work with that."

Aaru pulls a wheelie trolley with a big tub of sweet-smelling resin in it closer and gestures towards a set of brushes. I lean in and take two of them, handing one to Nik. His fingers brush against mine as he takes it, and we linger a moment longer than necessary. I never thought of us as particularly physically affectionate until now, but it's been hard to be near him and not touch very often, even if it's only in passing.

"We need to start by brushing the resin over the

linen, that will make sure it gets into all the dips and folds of the body, otherwise it risks air bubbles. Then we will transfer the body into the resin bath." He gestures to a large rectangular structure in the corner of the room that I've been dismissing as some kind of storage space.

It doesn't sound too complicated, I wonder why they haven't had us do this in London if it's this straightforward. We're allowed to make the resin mixture, so it isn't that they're worried about that.

Or maybe this is like the way Aaru wrapped the body. It's something they do here, but isn't how it's done back home. I suppose I'll find out at some point.

I hang back for a moment to see how Aaru uses his brush, only starting to apply the resin once I'm sure I'll do it right. I have no plans to start disrespecting Anubis by preparing the dead wrong, and not because I fear his wrath.

This is what I've wanted to do for my entire life, I'm not going to mess it up.

Chapter 11

Nik treks up the river bank towards me with Matia skipping around his legs. He's probably already started giving her scraps from the food he's bought us and he'll never be rid of her now. I'm reasonably sure that's why she's so connected to him, though a part of me has wondered whether it's more than that and Anubis is trying to tell us that Nik is also sort of Blessed. Not in the same way I am, I'm sure Nik would have noticed if he was able to use Blessed Sense, but in more of an approval way. I've heard rumours that the gods often show favour in a way that isn't quite Blessed but I don't know enough about it to be sure of how it works.

One part of me hopes he has that, because he deserves it. Another doesn't want it to be the case because I don't know what it would mean for our relationship if Anubis is the one who orchestrated the two of us meeting.

Maybe it doesn't really matter. Anubis can do many things, but I don't think he can control someone's heart. And if he chose us both, then it's because we both have qualities he deems desirable in his priests, which are probably something we both find attractive in another person too. Even without Anubis' input, we might still have ended up in exactly the same position.

Which is something I'm going to hold onto and believe as true.

"Here you go," Nik says, holding out a flatbread full to the brim with grilled meat and onions.

"Thanks, it smells much better than the stuff they're serving in the canteen."

He chuckles and sits down next to me, patting the ground so Matia comes to join us. She lies at his feet but doesn't close her eyes. She's too busy looking at him hopefully.

"I don't understand how they can serve that stuff, or why more of the priests aren't leaving for their evening meals," Nik admits.

A shudder runs down my spine at the thought

of eating another meal there. "I guess free food is still a draw, even if it's bad."

"Hmm. Maybe." He takes a bite of his flatbread and nods appreciatively. "This is good though."

I try my own, unsurprised to find he's telling the truth. We eat in relative silence, only exchanging comments about the food and how pleasant the breeze coming off the river is. I want to talk to him more, but I'm too hungry to be able to focus.

"Did you grow up here?" I ask Nik once I'm done eating.

He shakes his head. "But I visited a lot." He offers one of his remaining chunks of meat to Matia, who gobbles it up so fast I'm not sure she even tastes it. "Mum has a lot of family up here, so we'd come for a couple of days here and there. But most of the time, we stayed in London. I think Father preferred our trips to Egypt than here."

"Did you go often?"

"Not as often as Father would have liked. When I was a child he used to talk as if he personally knew Pharaoh Mentuhotep, but as I grew older, I realised that probably wasn't true and they only knew each other in a professional capacity."

"He seemed friendly with Ramesses." I watch his face closely as I say the prince's name, but he doesn't react the same way he would have done a few months ago. Being honest with him about what happened between me and Ramesses seems to have solved some of his jealousy issues.

"You'll probably know better than me, but I think that was mostly politics on both sides," Nik responds.

"Hmm, you have a point. Ramesses' threats were all about how he'd damage me politically." I try not to let the worry build up within me about that. I have no idea what Ramesses is planning to do, but it can't be good.

"So he's probably using Father for political leverage."

I let out a soft snort. "He's going to regret that when Ma'at's temple is finished with him. He's going to hate me even more if that happens."

"That's not your fault," Nik points out. "You're just doing your duty."

"I know." But that doesn't stop it being difficult to think about at times. Ramesses is a wild card that I don't know how to deal with, while Ma'at's priestesses are just terrifying. I know we're going to get called to the temple once we return to London, and then we're going to have to properly come to terms with the fact we've caused the London

Temple of Anubis to be investigated for wrongdoing.

Nik reaches out and puts an arm around me. I lean against him, settling my head on his shoulder and enjoying the comfort just being near him brings.

"I'm worried about what's happening in London," I admit.

"With Ma'at? I don't think they'll do much while we're gone, and even if they do, it isn't a bad thing. Maybe it'll all be over by the time we get back."

A small laugh bursts from me. "You really think an investigation from the goddess of justice's temple is going to be over in under a month?"

"I hate it when you're so logical," he teases.

"That's such a lie. You love it." Oops. Probably shouldn't say the l-word about anything right now, not until we're in that place.

"I do," he admits softly. "And I get it. You're worried about how much worse things could get while we're gone, but I think the answer is that the organ smuggling and the disappearing bodies were around long before we uncovered them. The people behind it are probably carrying on as if nothing has changed. And even if we were there, what would they care that a couple of junior priests have caught on to what they're doing? They'd probably just ignore us, or try to pay us off. Besides, if anything goes really badly, one of the others will message us about it. I know they don't know exactly how bad it is, but Hannu loves to gossip."

"Now you're the one using logic." I especially enjoy his point about Hannu telling us about anything that happens while we're gone. It didn't happen straight away, but there's no denying that the apprentices we joined the priesthood with are one unit. They'll look out for us while we're here, just like we've looked out for them in the past.

"And you love it just as much."

I chuckle. "I do," I echo his own words, noticing that he used the same ones I did. Perhaps we're more ready than I thought.

He rests his head on top of mine and takes a deep breath. "At least we're learning while we're here."

"It is an advantage. Though I'm worried for your aunt," I admit. "Most priests haven't even started learning traditional mummification by this point in their training, we're lucky Hori had already started us on it."

"Thank the gods for Hori," Nik agrees. "But I

wouldn't worry for my aunt. She's being prepared for burial by a Blessed, she'd have loved it."

"Did you know her well?"

He shakes his head. "Being here makes me remember her vaguely from family events, but she never really took an interest in me, and I never thought twice about all the relatives whose names I could barely recall."

Ah, yes. The complications of having a big family.

"We're doing a good job, Ani," he assures me. "And it's not like we're completely alone. The preparation priests have their jobs too, and Aaru is a decent guide."

"Do you think he's been asked to spy on us?"

"Maybe. Or he might just have been told to keep an eye on us to make sure we don't cause any trouble."

"Because of our reputation for it, or because they don't like that we've been sent here?"

"The latter, I think."

Matia sniffs the air as if she can smell something good. For a moment, I wonder if she's going to go investigate, but she seems to decide it isn't worth it and puts her head back down.

I lean forward to give her a couple of strokes.

I'm glad she got to come with us, though it would have been odd for me to turn up without her. Blessed animals are expected to go around with their human, it makes for good companionship, though I'm glad she's a jackal and not a lioness like the Blessed priestesses of Sekhmet would have following them around.

The breeze picks up into a slightly chill wind. A shiver runs down my spine and Nik pulls me closer.

"We should get back," he says.

"Just five more minutes." I'm enjoying the moment too much to want to end it quite yet, even if it's cold.

"Always, if I get to spend them with you," Nik says.

I laugh lightly and lean further into him. "That was smooth."

"It was meant to be," he says, kissing the top of my head.

The moment is a simple one, stolen from the middle of a busy few weeks while we do what we can to prepare his aunt for the afterlife. But it's perfect all the same.

Chapter 12

The common room is almost empty save for Neheb and his jackal sitting in the corner. Despite nearly a month passing since our arrival, I still haven't managed to talk to him. It's as if people are trying to keep him out of my way, though I don't know why they'd want to do that when I can help him. That should be at the top of everyone's agenda considering how little control he seems to have over his jackal, and how distressed the creature seems to be.

As if wanting to prove my point, Neheb's jackal jumps up at the table and grabs a piece of meat from his plate.

"Pakham, no," he scolds him. "Down." He sounds desperate.

I take a deep breath and head over to him with Matia trotting along beside me. The least I can do is help him form a better connection with his jackal, that way things won't continue to be unmanageable until Khafre arrives.

"Do you mind if I sit?" I ask, gesturing to the seat opposite him.

For a moment, I think he's going to say no, but eventually, he nods. The way he stares at me almost seems apprehensive. Though perhaps he's just vaguely intimidated by me being an older Blessed. Hopefully, I can do something about that.

I pull out the chair and sit down. To my surprise, Matia gives the other jackal a wide berth, something she's never done with Beni, the sacred jackal belonging to my Blessed mentor. She sits on the opposite side of me and eyes Pakham as if he's done something wrong, only serving to raise my suspicions. Matia is normally friendly with everyone she meets, if she doesn't like someone, then there's probably a good reason for that. I trust her judgement too much to ignore it.

"Are you having trouble forming your bond with him?" I ask, not bothering to make small talk. If I'm right about the other priests trying to keep the two of us apart, then there's a good chance I'm not going to be able to have much time alone with him.

Neheb glances around as if he's worried to talk to me without permission, only solidifying my decision.

"I'm not trying to interfere," I assure him quickly. "But I've been where you are, I might be able to help." Though I don't think I ever had this much trouble with Matia, she bonded to me pretty quickly, and I to her.

I reach down and scratch her ears, unsure whether she knows I'm thinking about her. She probably can, but I've never been clear on that part of having a Blessed animal.

"She's very well-behaved," Neheb says, looking at my jackal with a hint of jealousy in his eyes.

"She is. And Pakham can be too," I promise.

"I don't think that's going to be possible," he mutters.

"It will be. You just have to learn control. Khafre will be able to help you more when he arrives, but I might be able to give you a few pointers before then, if you want." I don't want him to feel pressured, but I can also see how much strain the current situation is putting him under and I definitely want to take some of that away from him.

Surprise flits across his face. "Why are you being so nice?" Something about the way he says it makes it feel like he's younger than eighteen. Or maybe it's more complicated than that. I don't know him well enough to be able to make a judgement about it.

"Why wouldn't I be? It's in my best interests." I shrug, truly baffled by why he might possibly think I wouldn't want to be nice. "We're both Blessed, that means we're going to have shared duties."

Panic flashes through his eyes. "Like what?"

"Honestly, I'm not sure yet, I've only been Blessed since last year. But there will be times when we're called on along with the other Blessed to perform duties, and there's the Festival of the Blessed at the end of the year too."

"Like if the Pharaoh dies?" Neheb asks.

"Probably." I try not to dwell on the fact that might bring me face-to-face with Ramesses again. At least he won't be the new Pharoah as his sister is the Crown Princess, which I'm sure he hates. I push thoughts of the prince to the side. It'll be years before the Pharaoh passes on to the afterlife, which is plenty of time for Ramesses to get over the fact I ended things between us and didn't wait for him to do the honours.

"All right, if you want to teach me..."

"Neheb," a commanding voice scolds. "What are you doing?"

I turn to see one of the priests in the doorway of the room.

"I-I was just eating, Priest Senbi," Neheb says, pointing to his empty plate.

"You have duties to attend to." He points out of the door.

I frown, wanting to say something, but unsure exactly what. No wonder Neheb feels younger than eighteen, he's being treated as if he's five. Is it because he's Blessed, or do they treat all the apprentices so badly here? I'm not sure which answer is better, and it makes me wish we had a trustworthy High Priest in command so I could report this.

"Come find me if you want my help," I say to Neheb, but I can already tell it's an offer he isn't going to take me up on.

He smiles weakly but doesn't say anything. He picks up a piece of meat from his tray and waves it in front of his jackal's face.

I frown. He shouldn't have to do that. I'm not against feeding the jackals treats or human food, but it shouldn't be needed to get them to do things.

"Pakham, come," Neheb says, luring the jackal away from the table with the piece of meat.

Matia lets out a small whine and cocks her head to the side, seemingly as confused as I am about the entire situation. Something about this isn't right.

I don't move the entire time, watching Neheb and his jackal leave while trying to work out what's so odd about the situation.

Senbi glares at me, clearly unhappy that I've done something as simple as talk to the temple's Blessed.

Thankfully, he chooses not to say anything to me and turns to leave.

Nik appears at that moment, his gaze flitting between me and the priest, already managing to put the pieces together.

He hurries over and drops into the chair beside me.

"I don't know," I say before he can even ask. "I saw Neheb struggling with Pakham again, and I came over to talk to him to see if I could help. The next thing I knew, Senbi was ordering him out of the room."

"He didn't look like he had any control over his jackal when I passed him outside," Nik responds, making sure to pat Matia as he does, only drawing attention to the fact that even he has more control over my jackal than Neheb has over his.

"He didn't in here either. He just lured Pakham away from the table with a piece of meat."

A frown pulls at Nik's handsome face. "Really?"

I nod.

"You never had to do that."

"I know. It makes me wonder..." I trail off, not knowing whether or not it's a good idea to say the words out loud.

"If he's Blessed at all?" Nik finishes for me.

"Yes. But I don't know if that's just my insecurities about having another Blessed around talking." There's a real chance all of this is coming from the wrong place.

"Hmm. Maybe? I do think it's strange that they won't let him talk to you though."

"It *is* strange. Hori apologised to me that it was taking so long to get another Blessed to come to the temple to train me when it was my turn. I know I'm nowhere near Khafre's level with my Blessed Sense, but it's weird that they won't let me help him. You'd have thought that would have been one of their conditions for letting us come."

"Hmm."

"What are you thinking?"

"How do you know I'm thinking of anything?"

I raise an eyebrow. "Because you've got your

thinking face on. I know you well enough to recognise it."

He chuckles. "I was wondering whether it would be worth it if you messaged Khafre to see when he's coming? He'll definitely be able to tell whether Neheb is the real deal or not."

"See, I knew you were thinking of something good," I point out.

The way he smiles at me makes my heart flutter. It's like there's a look he saves just for me, and I love it.

"I'll do it when we get back to the room," I say. Even though I only plan on messaging, I don't want to take the risk of someone looking over my shoulder and seeing that I don't trust their Blessed.

It'll be even more of a problem if they think Khafre isn't trustworthy when he arrives.

"Do you want to go out and get some food first?" Nik asks. "One of the priests told me about a restaurant I think you'll like."

"Are you asking me on a date, Nikare?" I tease.

"I don't know about that." There's a sparkle in his eye that reveals he's only messing with me.

"I guess we'll decide when we get there. Do we not have anything else we need to do here?"

He shakes his head. "I just did a last check on

the body, it should be ready for the funeral in a couple of days."

"What do we do until then?" I ask. "I'm guessing we can't go home."

"We can't," he responds. "So I guess we'll just take some time off."

I raise an eyebrow. "We've been bad at that over the past year."

"Of course we have. Why take time off when there's someone you want to spend every day with already at work."

My cheeks flush. "You can stop with the charm offensive now," I mutter.

"No charm, just truth," he promises. "I'm glad I get to spend my working time with you, but it's even better that I get to spend my days off with you too."

"I know the feeling. So let's start with food. We can make a plan for the next few days while we're eating." I get to my feet without waiting for him to respond.

We've been working hard, and we deserve a couple of days to decompress and relax away from the stress of temple life and everything that comes with it.

Chapter 13

The courtyard next to the burial site is filled with faces I vaguely recognise from the evening with Nik's family, and some that I don't. I've witnessed a lot of people preparing for funerals, but this is easily one of the biggest gatherings I've encountered so far, and that's without the priests.

Henutsen nods at me from her position near the head of the mourners, and I return the gesture, hoping this means that I've made a good impression on Nik's family. Even if I'm probably not going to see much of them, I want them to like me. And to think I'm good for Nik.

I straighten my head, trying to ignore the weight of my headdress. I'm not used to wearing one as I'm not senior enough in the priesthood to really be needed at any of the funerals in an official capacity, and certainly not as one of the participating priests. My experience of them so far has been mostly relegated to watching people get ready in the courtyards opposite the mortuary.

But this time is different. I'm visiting as a representative of the High Priest, and I'm the only Blessed in attendance.

Well, other than Neheb. But he's being kept far enough away from me that it's only adding to my suspicions of whether he truly is Blessed.

Hopefully, Khafre's arrival tomorrow will shed some light on the situation. Much to my relief, he's hastening his journey so he can check on the new Blessed sooner rather than later. I'm glad of it, though not in the slightest bit surprised. Khafre takes his role as mentor seriously, and when our lessons together ended, he promised he'd be there if I needed him.

High Priest Hunefer makes his way towards us, a displeased expression on his face that I don't think has anything to do with his attendance at a funeral.

"Priest Nikare," he greets Nik with a nod of his head.

Nik returns the gesture. "High Priest."

"Blessed Priestess Ankhesenamun."

"High Priest," I respond, only moving my head as far as I dare to. The last thing I want is for my headdress to fall off and make a scene.

"Are you ready for the Opening of the Mouth?" he asks.

I blink a couple of times, unsure what he means by that. No one has ever asked me if I'm ready to watch that before. Mostly because there isn't any need to, it's just a standard part of the ceremony, normally performed by the highest-ranking Priest of Anubis.

He gestures for a young man to come forward and present a cushion with the tools for the ceremony on them.

Which is when it dawns on me.

I'm the ranking priest. Kind of. Nik and I are sent as representatives of the High Priest in London, who outranks Hunefer, and being Blessed, I outrank Nik even if we're technically both at the same level according to the temple hierarchy.

"Would you give me a moment, High Priest? I want to properly prepare myself." My voice shakes as I speak, but I know I need to try and remain as calm as possible.

I step away and hurry around the side of the nearest building as panic starts to take hold. Matia chases after me on her somewhat gangly legs. In other circumstances, I may find her run amusing, but not right now.

"Ani? Are you okay?" Nik asks, having followed almost as swiftly.

I shake my head, instantly regretting it and putting my hand up to steady my headdress. "He wants me to do the Opening of the Mouth."

"So it seems."

A strangled squeak escapes me. "Shouldn't he be doing that?" Matia leans herself against my legs, offering me comfort in the way only she can. I reach down to touch her, wanting her to know how grateful I am that she's here.

"He could do it, but I think he's decided that he doesn't want to." Nik pulls a face that reveals exactly what he thinks of the High Priest's choice.

I close my eyes and try to think calming thoughts. "I've never done it before."

"You've practised on the dummy statues," he points out. "And you have your Blessed Sense."

I bite my lip and nod. He's not wrong. And Khafre did say that one of the things Blessed Sense helped with was this ceremony.

"I'll take the cushion with the implements, and I'll be right beside you the whole time, and so will

Matia," he promises. "You don't have to be alone for this."

That does make me feel a little better. "I wish Khafre could have arrived early."

"You'd still technically have outranked him when it comes to this."

"In which case, I wish temple politics made sense," I mutter.

Nik lets out a soft snort. "I wish that too."

"Let's get this over with. Is my headdress on straight?"

He reaches out and tucks a strand of hair behind my ear before fixing the headdress. "Now it is."

"Thanks, Nik."

"Anytime. Are you ready?"

I take a deep breath. "As ready as I can be."

With my head held high, I head back out to the waiting priests, not missing the smirk on High Priest Hunefer's face. There's no doubt he did this on purpose just to rattle me, though I'm not sure if it's because I'm female, because I'm Blessed, or because he dislikes that two junior priests outrank him today.

Probably the latter.

Nik picks up the leopard print robe one of the

priests is holding and gently drapes it across me. His gaze meets mine and I can see his belief in me. I need to hold onto that and not let Hunefer defeat me.

The robe smells musty, as if it hasn't been properly cared for. Or perhaps giving me one that has been out of use for a long time is another way for Hunefer to punish me. I refuse to let him know how much his actions are bothering me.

I tune out the wailing of the professional mourners as they throw themselves on the ground in front of the tomb while the family looks on. I'm not sure why they aren't doing this part themselves, normally mourners are only hired when it's the funeral of someone important, or if there are no family members to mourn, but it isn't my place to question it. Everything about this funeral has been a little over the top.

I move through them and stand at the entrance. I resist the urge to look at Nik for guidance. He's right, I've practised this even if I haven't done it properly myself.

Matia stands beside me with her head held high, but she doesn't demand any attention, unlike Neheb's jackal, who seems to be trying to make a break for it. I put the other Blessed and his predicament from my mind. I can't let myself get distracted when I have something as important as this to do. No matter what's going on in the temple, my duty is to Anubis and the dead first.

I close my eyes and send out my Blessed Sense. Priests who don't have it can still perform the Opening of the Mouth ceremony, but they need to inhale hallucinogenic incense in order to fall into the trance necessary for it, whereas I can reach out and feel the deceased around us.

"I have seen my father in all his forms," I announce, my voice only shaking slightly.

The other assembled priests begin to call on me to become one with Horus and protect the deceased.

I don't feel any different, but that's because I think this is mostly symbolic.

I take the ritual arm-shaped adze from Nik and touch it to the statue's ears, eyes, and mouth, opening them to the sights, sounds, and tastes that await them in the afterlife. Around me, the priests chant spells from the Book of the Dead, making the air around me pulse with the innate magic of life and death. I set down the adze and turn to Nik, who hands me a calf's leg and I take it gingerly, not wanting to get any of the blood on my formal clothing, or on the borrowed leopard print robe. I lift the bleeding stump to the statue's lips and then hand it back to Nik so I can wipe it off.

Despite the fact this is nothing but a stone effigy of the deceased, I can sense their soul bonding with it through my Blessed powers. It's unlike anything I've ever experienced before and I hope I can use that to guide me.

Grain and a peseshkaf blade are placed in the bowl to the front of the statue in an offering that will enter the tomb with it, signalling that the ceremony is complete.

The air vibrates with the echo of the woman's soul as she begins the next part of her life. She has a long journey ahead of her to get to Duat, but hopefully, we've prepared her in a way that will make it possible for her to pass without too much difficulty.

The atmosphere around us changes as she departs, and the other priests come forward to take the coffin and the statue into the tomb. I step back, knowing my work here is done and that I need to make space so they can seal the tomb.

"Thank you for your help," I say to Matia.

She lets out a soft yip, making me smile. She always knows what to say.

Nik makes his way over and reaches out to take

the borrowed robe from me. "You did great," he assures me. "I'd never have known it was your first time."

"You have to say that," I mutter.

"No, I don't. You know I wouldn't lie about your work, even if it would make you feel better."

I sigh. He's not wrong. I trust him to tell me the truth about that. He wants to displease Anubis almost as little as I do.

"Hunefer doesn't look happy," he says, glancing over at the High Priest. "I think he might have expected you to fail."

"Then he isn't a very good High Priest," I mutter. "Or maybe there's some kind of High Priest training they all do that stops them caring about the things that matter." I glance at the tomb, relieved that I managed the ceremony correctly, but frustrated by Hunefer's disregard for the deceased.

"We'll add it to our report to Ma'at's temple," Nik promises. "I know it's annoying, but we can't draw too much attention to it while we're working on something bigger."

I sigh. "I know. And I can't wait to go home, even if we have to deal with everything there."

"Me too. But first, we need to get to the funeral feast. They'll have roast beef."

Matia yips excitedly, though I think he was trying to convince me and not her with that.

"I'll feed you some under the table," he promises my jackal.

I shake my head in bemusement. "You spoil her."

"And you don't? I've seen your drawer of treats for her, and there are so many toys spread around the floor of your room that I sometimes worry I'm going to trip over one."

"Then you should watch where you're going," I tease. "But also, you bought her half of them." He's probably bought Matia more things than he's bought me, but I don't mind.

"Guilty as charged," he responds. "Come on, you can take your headdress off before the feast if we go now."

"Why didn't you start with that." It'll be a relief to take it off. The rest of my formal wear will have to stay, but I can do something involving hair beads instead of the uncomfortable headdress I didn't want to wear to begin with.

The three of us head back to the temple to get ready for the feast. It's going to be a long night, and it's best to be prepared.

Chapter 14

My head hurts a little from the amount of wine I drank last night. There's clearly been no expense spared for Satiah's funeral, which I should have guessed from the fact that they requested High Priest Ahmose to do the embalming, and the use of the traditional mummification method instead of one of the cheaper options. Everything about this entire process has been about the best. It's interesting to see, considering most of my career so far has been focused on the cheaper and more manageable options of embalming.

I hurry down the corridor despite the pain in my head, checking the doors to make sure I stop at the right one. I knew my hangover no longer mattered the moment I got the message that my mentor had arrived, and I didn't want to delay talking to Khafre any longer than I had to.

Though I should perhaps stop thinking of him as my mentor when we're technically both just Blessed now.

I push the thought aside. No matter how our positions within the Temple of Anubis change, I doubt I'll ever be able to think of him as anything other than my teacher. He's the person who first started explaining what being Blessed means, and what I can do with the powers I've been granted by our shared god.

I push open the door and step inside. The middle-aged man smiles the moment he sets eyes on me, and his jackal bounces over to say hello to Matia. The two of them bonded well during my training and I imagine she's glad to see her friend again.

Seeing the two of them interact only confirms how off things are with Neheb and Pakham. Matia should be playing with the other Blessed jackal at every chance she gets, rather than shying away from him and never interacting at all.

"Ani," Khafre says warmly. "How have you been?"

"Good," I respond, taking a seat opposite him.

"I did my first Opening of the Mouth ceremony yesterday."

"I heard, though I have to say I was surprised to find you doing one so soon."

"Not half as surprised as I was," I mutter.

He chuckles good-naturedly. "But I also heard that it went well. I'm not surprised, you've always had a good ability to listen to your Blessed Sense."

I glance down, unsure how to take the praise. "Thank you."

"Do you want something to drink?" he asks.

"Just some water would be good," I say quickly.

Khafre laughs. "The funeral feast?"

I nod. "I think I drank more than at the last wedding I went to."

"You'll get used to it," he promises, pouring me a glass of water.

"Or I'll learn how to not drink so much." I accept the drink from him and take a sip.

"I've always found that to be the best remedy for a hangover." He glances over to the two jackals who appear to be playing some kind of game together.

"It's Nik's fault, he kept topping up our glasses." I shake my head in bemusement.

"Ah, so things are going well with him?" He

seems genuinely interested, but that's not a surprise. He seems to like Nik.

I nod. "Thank you for your advice, it made things clearer for me." I think things between Nik and I would have turned out the same if Khafre hadn't given me unsolicited advice to go for it, but his words were appreciated nonetheless. "I'm sure he'll come by later, but he wanted to give us some time alone." A decision that's probably been influenced by the hangover he's dealing with himself. Though I have less pity for him when he's the one behind the filled glasses.

Khafre nods. "So we can talk about your suspicions."

"It might be nothing," I say quickly. "It's just a feeling."

"Anubis blesses us for a reason, Ani. If you have a feeling that something is off about Neheb and his jackal, then the chances are strong that our god is trying to tell you something."

"Sometimes I wish he'd just appear in my dreams," I mutter.

"I think he would only do that if you chose not to listen to him," Khafre responds kindly. He has a point. Anubis is a god who loves subtlety, and knowing how to read the signs is a skill. "Tell me more about Neheb and what's made you suspicious."

I let out a loud sigh, realising how flimsy my evidence is. "It's the fact I don't know anything really. I've been here for a month and I've barely talked to him at all. I'd have thought the High Priest would want me to give him some kind of guidance, especially because his jackal seems incapable of behaving. Is that even possible with a Blessed bond?" It's a relief to finally be able to ask the questions that have been playing on my mind since we arrived.

"It's possible," Khafre confirms. "But not common. Not many Blessed bond with their jackals quite as quickly as you did with Matia, for some it does take longer. The jackal shouldn't be misbehaving though."

"Matia doesn't like him either. She tries to put as much distance between them as possible." I take a sip of my water, glad to find it helps chase away some of the headache. "I did offer to try and help Neheb, but we were interrupted by one of the other priests and I never got a chance to tell him anything. I've barely seen him since."

"That *is* suspicious," he says. "As is how late I got the request to come and teach a new Blessed."

"Oh?" I hope he's going to elaborate on that, even if it's only to slate my curiosity.

"It's nothing really, just a suspicion, like you said. Most of the Blessed requests come through on the Day of Choosing even if the locations of new Blessed aren't announced the other temples for a few weeks. I had the message about you from High Priest Ahmose barely an hour after Matia chose you. But in this case, it came three days later."

"And that's unusual?"

"Very. The High Priests are supposed to submit their requests as soon as possible in case there end up being two Blessed in one jurisdiction in the same year."

"What would happen in that case?"

"One of the Blessed would study for a year at the other's temple. I did it about six years ago when there was a Blessed from Paris and Madrid at the same time."

"Which did you teach them at?" I'm just curious now, but it's something that may affect me in the future if I ever decide to go into Blessed Mentorship.

"Paris. It's slightly closer to Egypt, which is better if I need to be recalled to the main temple."

"I didn't realise you reported back there." I

frown, trying to work out what that means. "Do all Blessed report to Egypt?"

"No. It depends on our jobs. At the moment, you report to your London temple. If you take a job that involves more travelling, then you'll report to one of the temples in Egypt. Probably in Cairo, but it could be one of the others."

"Oh." I lean back in my seat. "I never realised."

"Most don't." He shrugs. "Luckily for this temple, there aren't any other Blessed this year, so I was able to come here despite the delay. But I'd already been dispatched to another job, which is why I wasn't here yet."

"Until I messaged."

He nods. "I was able to use that to get redirected. I should be thanking you for that, and Neheb certainly should."

"You're welcome?"

He smiles reassuringly at me. "Neheb should be along at any moment. I sent a request to meet him just after I sent yours."

"Is there a chance he won't come?" I ask.

"It seems unlikely. Most people are aware that a summons from a Blessed Priest isn't a request."

I raise an eyebrow. "I didn't realise we had that much power."

"It depends on the temple, and it's not something I suggest abusing," he warns me. "Not that I think you would."

"I'm glad you have faith in me."

He chuckles. "I'm a good teacher."

I'm about to agree with him when the door opens and a priest I don't recognise steps inside. His attention is pulled to the jackals, and when he looks back at us, it's clear he's nervous about whatever message he has to deliver.

"Blessed Priest Khafre, Blessed Priestess Ankhesenamun." He dips his head at each of us in turn. "I'm afraid High Priest Hunefer has denied your request for Apprentice Neheb to visit you for training."

My eyes widen.

"Thank you for telling me," Khafre says as he rises to his feet. "You can go now."

The man hesitates for a moment, then disappears.

"What are you thinking?" I ask.

"That we should go and see the High Priest and have a chat with him."

"Matia, come," I command.

She's almost instantly by my side, bringing Beni with her to stand by Khafre.

"What do you think is happening?" I ask my mentor.

"I suspect you may be right in your suspicions and we're too close to discovering the truth," he says.

"Wouldn't it be better if we go find Neheb first?" I ask. "If the High Priest figures out that you suspect something, then he'll send someone to make sure Neheb can't be found."

"Which will be as good as an admission," Khafre points out. "But I think you're right to suggest speaking to Neheb first, he's probably the one who will tell the truth about the situation first. Do you know where he'll be?"

I shake my head. "But he might be in the dining hall."

"Then let's try there first. We can pick up Nik on the way, I'm sure he's going to want to know how this ends," Khafre says with a wry smile.

"You make him sound so nosy."

Khafre chuckles. "Everyone who spent any time at the London temple knows that the two of you have a habit of finding trouble."

"It just keeps appearing," I murmur.

"Oh, I know. You're uncovering problems that have been going on in the temples for a long time.

You seem to have a knack for it." There's a deep-rooted affection in his tone, as well as a hint of admiration, as if he thinks our penchant for trouble is a useful thing.

"Which seems to be annoying just about everyone," I mutter as we set off down the corridor.

"Not everyone," he assures me. "And there's a good chance that this is what Anubis chose to bless you for. He saw the team you and Nik would make and wanted to use you to uncover some of the problems in his temple."

I frown. "Nik said something like that."

"Then he's a smart man." A small smile plays on Khafre's lips. "And one who knows that it's good to listen to gods over men."

Chapter 15

Despite having my Blessed mentor by my side, I feel more nervous than I should walking into the dining hall. Especially considering I've done nothing wrong and no one is even thinking that I have.

Unless Neheb truly is Blessed, in that case, I've created a fuss out of nothing. But considering Khafre seems to share my suspicions, and the High Priest doesn't want him to meet Neheb, that seems unlikely at this point.

I scan the room, relieved to find it mostly empty, but even more so to realise the other Blessed and his jackal are among the few people in there.

One of the many advantages of having Blessed animals is that I don't need to point him out to Khafre. Instead, my mentor approaches the table

Neheb sits at with Beni trotting along by his side. I follow a little more reluctantly, with Nik and Matia, neither of them seeming to know what to do either.

"May I?" Khafre asks, gesturing to Pakham.

"You can," Neheb says. "But I wouldn't."

A low growl comes from the jackal, warning Khafre not to touch him.

Beni lets out a whine, wanting to protect her human companion.

"It's okay," Khafre says, though I'm not sure which of the jackals he's talking to.

I glance at Nik, but he seems just as confused as I am about the situation. I don't know if that's reassuring or not. Sometimes it feels as if he knows more than anyone about the priesthood, having grown up his entire life around it, so his not knowing something is a little off-putting.

Khafre places his hand on Pakham's head and the jackal lets out a sad whimper.

My heart aches for him. If he's been behaving as badly as he has been since the Day of Choosing, it can't have been a very fun few months for him. I reach down to touch the top of Matia's head to reassure myself she's okay. She leans against my leg, seeming to realise I need the reassurance.

"Thank you, Pakham," Khafre says as he

straightens up. "Neheb, I think you should come with us," he says to the apprentice, not unkindly.

"I-I don't think the High Priest would like that." Fear crosses over his features.

"I think the High Priest would like it even less if we talked about your secret here," Khafre says, not unkindly.

Neheb swallows and looks around before deciding it really is in his best interests to comply.

Khafre gestures for Nik and exchanges a few quiet words with him, though I'm not close enough to be able to tell what they're saying. Nik nods and leaves the room without a moment's hesitation. I want to ask where he's going, but I don't think it's the right time to. We have to play this just right if we want to get to the bottom of the situation with Neheb.

Khafre leads us from the dining hall and to a private chamber while the three jackals follow behind. Beni is doing the same thing as Matia and putting distance between them and poor Pakham. He trails along slowly, seemingly chastised about something, but I'm not sure what. I wish there was something I could do to make the jackal more at ease, but I'm clueless, never having dealt with a situation like this before.

"Take a seat," Khafre says once the three of us are alone.

Neheb sits gingerly on the edge of one of the chairs, while I sit next to Khafre and wait for the older man to say something. There's no doubt in my mind that he's the one in charge right now, and I'm glad of it. I don't have enough experience to feel comfortable in that role.

"The High Priest will probably be along shortly," Khafre says. "So why don't we cut to the chase? Are you really Blessed, Neheb?"

"No." The word is barely above a whisper, but I definitely hear it. From the expression on Khafre's face, so did he.

I blink a couple of times, having expected him to at least try and deny it.

"I knew you'd figured it out," Neheb says, looking at me with a mournful expression. "When you asked me if I wanted your help."

"I meant it," I respond. "And I didn't suspect you until you didn't come to find me."

"You can't help me," Neheb says, looking down at the ground as tears pool in his eyes.

Despite the lies he's told, I feel sorry for him. Anyone with eyes should be able to see that he's not the mastermind behind this.

"We can." Khafre moves over to sit down next to him and offers him a reassuring pat on the shoulder. "But you need to tell us what happened. We've sent for the priests from Ma'at's temple, so what you say will make a difference to what happens to you."

Ah, so that's where he sent Nik.

"There's no escaping this, is there?" Neheb's eyes are wide and panicked, making him even younger than normal.

"You tried to deceive Anubis, so no," I respond bluntly.

"It wasn't my idea." There's a hint of desperation in his voice that reveals he might be telling the truth. "My family is struggling. My dad broke his arm and got fired from his job, then my mum left him and we had to figure out how to take care of my siblings. Then High Priest Hunefer came to the house and said that he'd pay us if I hid a piece of chicken in my robes on the Day of Choosing. It was a lot of money and I couldn't really say no. I didn't expect Pakham to walk up to me, or for anyone to start saying I was Blessed. The next thing I knew, I was here with a jackal who can't stand me, not able to do anything about it. Was he going to make me lie my entire life?"

"That wouldn't have been possible," Khafre

says. "All it took was a few encounters with Ani for her to start suspecting, and I confirmed it within a moment through your lack of bond with Pakham. You'd have been found out as soon as you came into contact with another Blessed, or if you had to do something that requires someone with access to the powers. I'm afraid to say that you've been used by someone who was probably going to blame it all on you."

Neheb slumps back in his seat. "Will my family get to keep the money?" he asks.

"I don't know," Khafre responds. "That will be up to the Temple of Ma'at."

The door bursts open and the three of us turn to see High Priest Hunefer barging in with his face red with barely contained anger. "What is going on here?" he demands.

Khafre rises to his feet and holds out his hand. "Good morning, you must be High Priest Hunefer."

"And who are you?" he snaps.

"I'm Blessed Priest Khafre, you'll have been told of my arrival, I'm sure."

Hunefer's gaze darkens. "I told you that Neheb would not be seeing you."

"So you did. And that made me wonder why,

especially when there is already a Blessed Priestess visiting your temple."

Hunefer glares at me as if it's my fault that I was sent here.

"We know the truth, High Priest. I suggest that you ready yourself for your departure," Khafre says.

"I'm not going anywhere. You are insulting me, and my Blessed, with your vague insinuations," he huffs.

"Very well. I believe you paid Apprentice Neheb to pretend to be Blessed because you wanted the prestige that it brought to the temple to have one." No matter how angry the other man is, Khafre keeps his voice level and his words clear. I hope to reach his level of calm one day. "The Temple of Ma'at has been informed."

"We've done nothing wrong," Hunefer responds sharply.

"That is for them to decide. If you're telling the truth, then you have nothing to worry about." He nods towards the doors where two priestesses with steely gazes have just appeared, followed by a rather nervous-looking Nik. I don't blame him. I'm not sure what they teach the apprentices in Ma'at's temple, but her priestesses always turn out to be formidable.

"High Priest Hunefer, Apprentice Neheb, we have reason to suspect that you have falsely and knowingly defrauded the Temple of Anubis," the priestess on the right says. "You will come with us for questioning."

Neheb is on his feet within seconds and makes his way over to the woman with a look of relief on his face. He's probably glad that this is all over.

Hunefer looks as if he's about to explode, but I don't think he can when there are so many witnesses.

"Fine," he says sharply. "But you'll regret this." I'm not sure which of us his comment is aimed at, but considering he's guilty and the priestesses can tell when someone lies to them, I don't think he's going to find this as easy as he thinks he's going to.

"Please come to the temple this afternoon," one of the priestesses says to us.

"We will," Khafre assures her.

The four of them disappear through the temple and back to the outside world.

Khafre sighs, a slightly amused expression on his face. "Well, you two really do know how to sniff out trouble," he jokes with us. "At least this time we were able to get it sorted."

"What will happen now?" Nik asks.

"The same thing that happens every time someone tries this, which is more often than you think. Hunefer will find himself demoted or completely removed from the temple, along with a hefty fine. Neheb will probably be let go with a warning and no reference, but he won't be able to work in any of the other temples either, but he should be fine to get a job as a craftsman or doing anything else."

"It seems harsh when he's been used."

"Maybe. But he had chances to speak up about it and chose not to," Khafre points out.

"What about Pakham?" Nik asks.

I glance in the direction of the poor jackal, who is still being kept at a distance by Matia and Beni.

"I think it would be best if he's sent to one of the jackal handlers somewhere other than York. This has been a stressful experience for him and he needs a chance to recuperate from it. Do you know if Inkaef has space in London?"

"I think so, it's been a while since I needed to go to visit though, so things might have changed," I say.

Khafre nods. "I'll send a message to him and arrange everything. Even if he doesn't have space, I'm sure he'll know someone that does. But the two of you shouldn't linger here in case things go badly."

Nik nods. "We're leaving for London this evening."

"Good. Go to Ma'at's temple now and give your statements, then try to leave as soon as possible."

I nod, knowing he's right. "Will we see you there?"

"Yes. I'll be along as soon as I've sent the message to Inkaef. We can save our goodbyes until then."

A wave of sadness flows through me at the idea of leaving my Blessed mentor's company again so soon, but I know this is the way of things. And that our paths will cross in the future too.

"Come on," Nik says. "The sooner we get this over with, the better."

I nod, trying to cover up my nerves over going to Ma'at's temple. At least it will give us an excuse if they call us when we're back down in London too.

Maybe I should have been Blessed by Ma'at instead of Anubis.

Chapter 16

"Please, sit down," the priestess says, gesturing to the seat. "I see from your records that you've testified with us before?"

I nod as I sit down, taking a moment to ensure Matia is comfortable next to me. "Yes, it was in London."

"Excellent. Then you know what to expect. I can tell when you lie, which makes your testimony valuable. Can you please state your name?" She gestures for the priest in the corner to start taking notes.

I clear my throat. "I'm Ankhesenamun. Sorry, Blessed Priestess Ankhesenamun of the Temple of Anubis."

"Very good. Now, why don't you tell us what

happened in regards to Apprentice Neheb," she says.

I start at the beginning, doing my best not to leave anything important out, while not revealing anything about mine and Nik's existing dealings with Ma'at's temple. I'm sure the priestess has access to those on my records too, but there's a chance this testimony will be shown to High Priest Ahmose, and the last thing we want is for him to get wind of the investigation we've started into the way he runs his temple.

The priestess nods along, asking me the odd question, but mostly letting me speak in my own words. My mouth grows dry from all the talking, but I push through.

"And then you came to take them away," I finish.

She nods. "Thank you. Your testimony has been recorded. Please follow me." She gets to her feet and indicates for me to do the same.

A small part of me feels a little underwhelmed by how simple the testimony actually is, but perhaps I'm just getting used to being around Ma'at priests.

Nik's whole face lights up when he sees me and Matia coming out of the room and he hurries over. "Are you done?"

"I think so." I check with the priestess, who nods.

"We're just waiting on Khafre, then we can go," Nik says. "Or do we need to stay in York?" he asks the priestess.

"You're fine to return to London," she says, almost kindly. "And our Blessed there send their regards to you both."

I smile uneasily, trying not to look at Nik and give us away. "Thank you."

She nods. "Farewell for now."

"Dare I ask what that was about?" Khafre asks from behind us.

I jump and turn around, trying not to look too guilty. "Would you believe me if I said I didn't know?"

A small smile curls at my mentor's lips as he reaches down and scratches the top of Beni's head, getting a satisfied whine from his jackal as a response. "I think you know the answer to that."

"Then I know what it was about, but I can't tell you," I admit, hating lying to my mentor, even if it is through omission. I'm sure he'll find out in time, if he hasn't already put the pieces together.

"And you, Nik?" he asks, a hint of amusement in his tone.

"I can't say."

He studies the two of us intently, with an expression I can't quite place on his face, almost as if he's trying to work something out. "Then you shouldn't tell me."

I frown. "You're just going to trust us after all of this?" I wave my hand around the table.

Khafre chuckles. "I've had the honour of teaching you, Ani. I know you well enough to be certain what you're doing is for the good of the temple. I trust that the two of you know what you're doing."

"With the Temple of Ma'at, I'm not sure anyone does," I mutter.

Khafre chuckles. "You may not be wrong there."

"They came very quickly when you asked for them."

"They did," he acknowledges. "I have a history with the temple."

"That sounds ominous. But you're not going to tell me more about it, are you?"

He chuckles. "Not today, no. Remember when I told you that you had a lot still to learn about being Blessed?"

"Of course. Is this one of those things?" His

words are rather intriguing, but I can tell from his expression that he isn't going to tell me anything else, even if I prompt him to.

"It might be," he responds cryptically. "And if it is, then I look forward to teaching it to you."

"That's very cryptic."

"As were your responses. But if the two of you are up to what I think you're up to, then I believe you'll find out soon enough," Khafre says.

"Now you're just trying to confuse me," I murmur.

"I promise, I'm not. And I also promise that if you need my help, I'll be there to lend it to you, no questions asked," Khafre says.

"That's a dangerous offer."

"Not when I'm certain the three of us want the same things," he responds. "Unless you've changed your minds and don't want to serve our god."

"We haven't," Nik says quickly. "Honouring Anubis and the dead is our first priority."

"Then you have my help," Kafre responds. "But you should get going, your car will be here shortly."

"And I need to finish packing," I admit. "I didn't get a chance earlier."

"Is this what I'm going to have to put up with for the rest of my life?" Nik says offhandedly.

"Yes," I respond simply, while Khafre tries to smother a laugh.

"If Inkaef has space for Pakham, I'll see you there later this week. If not, then I'm not sure when it will be, but hopefully soon," he says.

"Thank you for all your help, Khafre," I say, and I mean it. I wouldn't have known how to test Neheb's jackal like that. I'm sure it's something I'll learn to do in time, but for now, I'm glad I can rely on my mentor for help when I need it.

"Any time, Ani."

It's sad to say goodbye to him again after so little time together, but I know he's right. We've done what we came to York to do, and we've managed to meddle with the temple affairs here in the process.

We really can't seem to stay out of trouble.

Epilogue

I'm more relieved than I want to admit about being back in our own temple, especially because there aren't as many people here who actively want us to leave it.

I unlock my door and push it open.

Matia bounces up onto my bed the moment we step through the door. I keep promising myself that I'm going to teach her not to sleep there, but I never get around to it. There's something comforting about having her around and knowing that she's close.

"You've got me well and truly wrapped around your paws, don't you?" I ask Matia.

Nik chuckles as he sets my bag down for me. "I think she has us all wrapped there."

"Mmm, that's the problem," I joke. "Thank you for bringing that in, you didn't have to."

"Maybe I just wanted to make my way into your room."

I let out a small snort. "Because you've *never* been in my room before."

"Nope, not at all. Ask anyone, I've never been in here before."

I roll my eyes. "You're being ridiculous."

"And you love it. That's part of my charm."

I step closer to him and he instantly wraps his arms around my waist, pulling me closer to him. I rest a hand on his chest and look up at him, taking a moment to enjoy the intimacy. It's only then that I realise just how hard our trip to York was on that front. Our relationship is still too new for us to know exactly how to act, but we normally get to have more time just for ourselves.

"Ani," Nik says.

"Hmm?"

"What's that?" he asks.

A frown pulls at my eyebrows. "What's what?"

"That. It looks like a letter of some kind."

I pull away from him and turn to look in the same direction as he is. Sure enough, a letter sits on the floor as if it's been slipped under the door.

I break away from Nik and pick it up, turning it over in my hands and noticing the feather seal on the other side.

"Ani?" he prompts.

"It's from Ma'at's temple," I whisper.

"And they delivered it here?" Panic fills his voice. "While we weren't around."

"Apparently." I sit down on the bed and turn it over in my hands a few more times without opening it.

Matia sniffs the letter, but decides it isn't interesting and flops down behind me.

"What's it say?" Nik goes over to the door and locks it without me having to ask him to. It seems unlikely that anyone is going to walk in on us, but it's always better to be safe rather than sorry, especially when it's something that could shake the entire temple and change the world as we know it.

Apparently, I'm feeling a little dramatic today. But after the past month, I think that makes sense.

I tear open the letter and scan the hieroglyphics within. "It's just a summons." I hold it out to him so he can read it himself. While it's in my room, it's addressed to both of us. Probably because Nik lives in the High Priest's house with his father, the main person the Temple of Ma'at is going to be investigating. I hope he's right about moving into the shared apartments soon, it'll make things a lot easier.

"What do you think they want from us?" Nik asks.

I shrug. "An update? To tell us that we're going to need to do something dangerous or reckless. At this point, I'm not really sure."

"At least the speculating will be over?"

"That's true." But for some reason, that's not as reassuring as it should be. Perhaps because I know that what comes next is going to be difficult.

But we're strong enough to do this. The corruption in the temple needs to be stopped or we'll all end up with our hearts deemed unworthy and eaten by Ammit before we can get to the afterlife. That's not how I want my existence to end.

Nik puts his arm around me and pulls me close, offering me strength when I otherwise feel like I have none. "It'll be okay," he promises.

"I hope you're right." Because if this goes badly, neither of us are going to have a job any more, and I'll be the first Blessed Priestess to be stripped of my position.

I'm determined not to let that happen. Whatever Ma'at's priestesses want, I'll do it. Especially if it means we can make our temple a better and more trustworthy place. The reward is worth the risk.

I hope.

Thank you for reading *Secrets Of The Chosen*, I hope you enjoyed it. If you want to continue the series, you can in *Priestess Of The Tombs:* https://books.authorlauragreenwood.co.uk/priestessofthetombs

You can also download a bonus scene of Nik and Neffie talking in the mortuary before Ani arrives for free here: https://books.authorlauragreenwood.co.uk/5lfwrp7fgd

Author Note

Thank you for reading *Secrets Of The Chosen*, I hope you enjoyed it!

This book sneaked up on me even more than *Priestess Of The Tombs* did. I actually first wrote *Secrets Of The Chosen* as a side story for Ani and Nik, but then Arizona read the story and informed me that she thought I should add a few more scenes and make it into a full book in the series...so here we are! Another unplanned book for Nik and Ani (which I suspect is not going to be the last, they're very talkative as characters).

You may wonder why I picked York as the place for the temple in this one. There are two reasons - the first is that it is a city that was founded by the Romans because of its location, and as the

Author Note

Egyptian Empire takes the place of the Roman Empire in this world, it seemed likely they would keep a city in the same spot. The second reason is a lot more personal, it's near where I grew up. I've been visiting York for longer than I can actually remember, which makes it fun for me to think of how it would be changed by the influence of the Egyptian Empire on the world.

The Opening of the Mouth ceremony is based on the information available about the real ancient ceremony (added with a bit of Blessed magic), though the ceremony would normally be performed by a specialised priest instead of a Blessed.

And finally, if you're wanting some other Egyptian mythology-inspired titles to read while you're waiting for more in *The Apprentice Of Anubis* series, why not check out one of my other series - *Forgotten Gods* or *The Queen Of Gods*, or my stand-alone Egyptian mythology paranormal romance, *Bastet*.

If you want to keep up to date with new releases and other news, you can join my Facebook Reader Group or mailing list.

Stay safe & happy reading!

- Laura

Get A Free Apprentice Of Anubis Story

When Neffie switches shifts with another one of Bastet's priestesses, the last thing she expects is to lose one of the sacred cats.

With her job on the line, she embarks on a mission across London to try and find the cat.

Can she find it before she earns the eternal displeasure of her goddess?

-

Feline Of Mourning is a standalone companion story to The Apprentice Of Anubis series, a modern fantasy set in an alternative version of London where the Egyptian Empire never fell.

Get A Free Apprentice Of Anubis Story

Feline Of Mourning can be read as a standalone. The events take place between chapters 3 & 4 of Secrets Of The Chosen.

You can download Feline Of Mourning for free here: https://books.authorlauragreenwood.co.uk/neffie

Also by Laura Greenwood

You can find out more about each of my series on my website.

- Obscure Academy: a paranormal romance series set at a university-age academy for mixed supernaturals. Each book follows a different couple.
- The Apprentice Of Anubis: an urban fantasy series set in an alternative world where the Ancient Egyptian Empire never fell. It follows a new apprentice to the temple of Anubis as she learns about her new role.
- Forgotten Gods: a paranormal adventure romance series inspired by Egyptian mythology. Each book follows a different Ancient Egyptian goddess.
- Amethyst's Wand Shop Mysteries (with Arizona Tape): an urban fantasy murder mystery series following a witch who teams up with a detective to solve murders. Each book includes a different murder.
- Grimm Academy: a fantasy fairy tale academy series. Each book follows a different fairy tale heroine.

- Jinx Paranormal Dating Agency: a paranormal romance series based on worldwide mythology where paranormals and deities take part in events organised by the Jinx Dating Agency. Each book follows a different couple.
- Purple Oasis (with Arizona Tape): a paranormal romance series based at a sanctuary set up after the apocalypse. Each book follows a different couple.
- Speed Dating With The Denizens Of The Underworld (shared world): a paranormal romance shared world based on mythology from around the world. Each book follows a different couple.
- Blackthorn Academy For Supernaturals (shared world): a paranormal monster romance shared world based at Blackthorn Academy. Each book follows a different couple.

You can find a complete list of all my books on my website:

https://books.authorlauragreenwood.co.uk/book-list

Signed Paperback & Merchandise:

You can find signed paperbacks, hardcovers, and merchandise based on my series (including stickers, magnets, face masks, and more!) via my website:

https://books.authorlauragreenwood.co.uk/shop

About Laura Greenwood

Laura is a USA Today Bestselling Author of paranormal romance, urban fantasy, and fantasy romance. When she's not writing, she drinks a lot of tea, tries to resist French macarons, and works towards a diploma in Egyptology. She lives in the UK, where most of her books are set. Laura specialises in quick reads, with healthy relationships and consent-positive moments regardless of if she's writing light-hearted romance, mythology-heavy urban fantasy, or anything in between.

Follow Laura Greenwood

- Website: www.authorlaura-greenwood.co.uk
- Mailing List: https://books.authorlauragreenwood.co.uk/newsletter
- Facebook Group: http://facebook.com/groups/theparanormalcouncil
- Facebook Page: http://facebook.com/authorlauragreenwood

- Bookbub: https://www.bookbub.com/authors/laura-greenwood